The Michael Moorcock Collection

The Michael Moorcock Collection is the definitive library of acclaimed author Michael Moorcock's SF & fantasy, including the entirety of his Eternal Champion work. It is prepared and edited by John Davey, the author's long-time bibliographer and editor, and will be published, over the course of two years, in the following print omnibus editions by Gollancz, and as individual eBooks by the SF Gateway (see http://www.sfgateway.com/authors/m/moorcock-michael/ for a complete list of available eBooks).

A Cornelius Calendar
comprising –
*The Adventures of Una Persson
and Catherine Cornelius in
the Twentieth Century*
The Entropy Tango
The Great Rock 'n' Roll Swindle
The Alchemist's Question
*Firing the Cathedral/Modem
Times 2.0*

Von Bek
comprising –
*The War Hound and the World's
Pain*
The City in the Autumn Stars

The Eternal Champion
comprising –
The Eternal Champion
Phoenix in Obsidian
The Dragon in the Sword

The Dancers at the
End of Time
comprising –
An Alien Heat
The Hollow Lands
The End of all Songs

Kane of Old Mars
comprising –
Warriors of Mars
Blades of Mars
Barbarians of Mars

Moorcock's Multiverse
comprising –
The Sundered Worlds
The Winds of Limbo
The Shores of Death

The Nomad of Time
comprising –
The Warlord of the Air
The Land Leviathan
The Steel Tsar

Travelling to Utopia
comprising –
The Wrecks of Time
The Ice Schooner
The Black Corridor

The War Amongst the Angels
comprising –
Blood: A Southern Fantasy
Fabulous Harbours
The War Amongst the Angels

Tales From the End of Time
comprising –
Legends from the End of Time
Constant Fire
Elric at the End of Time

Behold the Man

Gloriana; or, The Unfulfill'd Queen

SHORT FICTION
My Experiences in the Third World
War and Other Stories: The Best
Short Fiction of Michael Moorcock
Volume 1

The Brothel in Rosenstrasse and
Other Stories: The Best Short Fiction
of Michael Moorcock Volume 2

Breakfast in the Ruins and Other
Stories: The Best Short Fiction of
Michael Moorcock Volume 3

Introduction to
The Michael Moorcock Collection
John Clute

H E IS NOW over 70, enough time for most careers to start and end in, enough time to fit in an occasional half-decade or so of silence to mark off the big years. Silence happens. I don't think I know an author who doesn't fear silence like the plague; most of us, if we live long enough, can remember a bad blank year or so, or more. Not Michael Moorcock. Except for some worrying surgery on his toes in recent years, he seems not to have taken time off to breathe the air of peace and panic. There has been no time to spare. The nearly 60 years of his active career seems to have been too short to fit everything in: the teenage comics; the editing jobs; the pulp fiction; the reinvented heroic fantasies; the Eternal Champion; the deep Jerry Cornelius riffs; NEW WORLDS; the 1970s/1980s flow of stories and novels, dozens upon dozens of them in every category of modern fantastika; the tales of the dying Earth and the possessing of Jesus; the exercises in postmodernism that turned the world inside out before most of us had begun to guess we were living on the wrong side of things; the invention (more or less) of steampunk; the alternate histories; the *Mitteleuropean* tales of sexual terror; the deep-city London riffs: the turns and changes and returns and reconfigurations to which he has subjected his oeuvre over the years (he expects this new Collected Edition will fix these transformations in place for good); the late tales where he has been remodelling the intersecting worlds he created in the 1960s in terms of twenty-first-century physics: for starters. If you can't take the heat, I guess, stay out of the multiverse.

His life has been full and complicated, a life he has exposed and hidden (like many other prolific authors) throughout his work. In *Mother London* (1988), though, a nonfantastic novel published at what is now something like the midpoint of his career, it may be possible to find the key to all the other selves who made the 100 books. There are three protagonists in the tale, which is set from about 1940 to about 1988 in the suburbs and inner runnels of the vast metropolis of Charles Dickens and Robert Louis Stevenson. The oldest of these protagonists is Joseph Kiss, a flamboyant self-advertising fin-de-siècle figure of substantial girth and a fantasticating relationship to the world: he is Michael Moorcock, seen with genial bite as a kind of G.K. Chesterton without the wearying punch-line paradoxes. The youngest of the three is David Mummery, a haunted introspective half-insane denizen of a secret London of trials and runes and codes and magic: he too is Michael Moorcock, seen through a glass, darkly. And there is Mary Gasalee, a kind of holy-innocent and survivor, blessed with a luminous clarity of insight, so that in all her apparent ignorance of the onrushing secular world she is more deeply wise than other folk: she is also Michael Moorcock, Moorcock when young as viewed from the wry middle years of 1988. When we read the book, we are reading a book of instructions for the assembly of a London writer. The Moorcock we put together from this choice of portraits is amused and bemused at the vision of himself; he is a phenomenon of flamboyance and introspection, a poseur and a solitary, a dreamer and a doer, a multitude and a singleton. But only the three Moorcocks in this book, working together, could have written all the other books.

It all began – as it does for David Mummery in *Mother London* – in South London, in a subtopian stretch of villas called Mitcham, in 1939. In early childhood, he experienced the Blitz, and never forgot the extraordinariness of being a participant – however minute – in the great drama; all around him, as though the world were being dismantled nightly, darkness and blackout would descend, bombs fall, buildings and streets disappear; and in the morning, as though a new universe had taken over from the old one and the world had become portals, the sun would rise on glinting rubble, abandoned tricycles, men and women going about their daily tasks as though nothing had happened, strange shards of ruin poking into altered air. From a very early age, Michael Moorcock's security reposed in a sense that everything might change, in the blinking of an eye, and be *rejourneyed* the next day (or the next book). Though as a writer he has certainly elucidated the fears and alarums of life in Aftermath Britain, it does seem that his very early years were marked by the epiphanies of war, rather than the inflictions of despair and beclouding amnesia most adults necessarily experienced. After the war ended, his parents separated, and the young Moorcock began to attend a pretty wide variety of schools, several of which he seems to have been expelled from, and as soon as he could legally do so he began to work full time, up north in London's heart, which he only left when he moved to Texas (with intervals in Paris) in the early 1990s, from where (to jump briefly up the decades) he continues to cast a Martian eye: as with most exiles, Moorcock's intensest anatomies of his homeland date from after his cunning departure.

But back again to the beginning (just as though we were rimming a multiverse). Starting in the 1950s there was the comics and pulp work for Fleetway Publications; there was the first book (*Caribbean Crisis*, 1962) as by Desmond Reid, co-written with his early friend the artist James Cawthorn (1929–2008); there was marriage, with the writer Hilary Bailey (they divorced in 1978), three children, a heated existence in the Ladbroke Grove/Notting Hill Gate region of London he was later to populate with Jerry Cornelius and his vast family; there was the editing of NEW WORLDS, which began in 1964 and became the heartbeat of the British New Wave two years later as writers like Brian W. Aldiss and J.G. Ballard, reaching their early prime, made it into a tympanum, as young American writers like Thomas M. Disch, John T. Sladek, Norman Spinrad and Pamela Zoline found a home in London for material they could not publish in America, and new British writers like M. John Harrison and Charles Platt began their careers in its pages; but before that there was Elric. With *The Stealer of Souls* (1963) and

Stormbringer (1965), the multiverse began to flicker into view, and the Eternal Champion (whom Elric parodied and embodied) began properly to ransack the worlds in his fight against a greater Chaos than the great dance could sustain. There was also the first SF novel, *The Sundered Worlds* (1965), but in the 1960s SF was a difficult nut to demolish for Moorcock: he would bide his time.

We come to the heart of the matter. Jerry Cornelius, who first appears in *The Final Programme* (1968) – which assembles and co-ordinates material first published a few years earlier in NEW WORLDS – is a deliberate solarisation of the albino Elric, who was himself a mocking solarisation of Robert E. Howard's Conan, or rather of the mighty-thew-headed Conan created for profit by Howard epigones: Moorcock rarely mocks the true quill. Cornelius, who reaches his first and most telling apotheosis in the four novels comprising *The Cornelius Quartet*, remains his most distinctive and perhaps most original single creation: a wide boy, an agent, a *flaneur*, a bad musician, a shopper, a shapechanger, a trans, a spy in the house of London: a toxic palimpsest on whom and through whom the *zeitgeist* inscribes surreal conjugations of 'message'. Jerry Cornelius gives head to Elric.

The life continued apace. By 1970, with NEW WORLDS on its last legs, multiverse fantasies and experimental novels poured forth; Moorcock and Hilary Bailey began to live separately, though he moved, in fact, only around the corner, where he set up house with Jill Riches, who would become his second wife; there was a second home in Yorkshire, but London remained his central base. *The Condition of Muzak* (1977), which is the fourth Cornelius novel, and *Gloriana; or, The Unfulfill'd Queen* (1978), which transfigures the first Elizabeth into a kinked Astraea, marked perhaps the high point of his career as a writer of fiction whose font lay in genre or its mutations – marked perhaps the furthest bournes he could transgress while remaining within the perimeters of fantasy (though *within* those bournes vast stretches of territory remained and would, continually, be explored). During these years he sometimes wore a leather jacket constructed out of numerous patches of varicoloured material, and it sometimes seemed perfectly fitting that he bore the semblance, as his jacket flickered and fuzzed from across a room or road, of an illustrated man, a map, a thing of shreds and patches, a student fleshed from dreams. Like the stories he told, he seemed to be more than one thing. To use a term frequently applied (by me at least) to twenty-first-century fiction, he seemed equipoisal: which is to say that, through all his genre-hopping and genre-mixing and genre-transcending and genre-loyal returnings to old pitches, *he was never still*, because 'equipoise' is all about *making stories move*. As with his stories, he cannot be pinned down, because he is not in one place. In person and in his work, it has always been sink or swim: like a shark, or a dancer, or an equilibrist...

The marriage with Jill Riches came to an end. He married Linda Steele in 1983; they remain married. The Colonel Pyat books, *Byzantium Endures* (1981), *The Laughter of Carthage* (1984), *Jerusalem Commands* (1992) and *The Vengeance of Rome* (2006), dominated these years, along with *Mother London*. As these books, which are non-fantastic, are not included in the current *Michael Moorcock Collection*, it might be worth noting here that, in their insistence on the irreducible difficulty of gaining anything like true sight, they represent Moorcock's mature modernist take on what one might call the rag-and-bone shop of the world itself; and that the huge ornate postmodern edifice of his multiverse *loosens* us from that world, gives us room to breathe, to juggle our strategies for living – allows us ultimately to escape from prison (to use a phrase from a writer he does not respect, J.R.R. Tolkien, for whom the twentieth century was a prison train bound for hell). What Moorcock may best be remembered for in the end is the (perhaps unique) interplay between modernism and postmodernism in his work. (But a plethora of discordant understandings makes these terms hard to use; so enough of them.) In the end, one might just say that Moorcock's work as a whole represents an extraordinarily multifarious execution of the fantasist's main task: which is to *get us out of here*.

Recent decades saw a continuation of the multifarious, but with a more intensely applied methodology. The late volumes of the long Elric saga, and the Second Ether sequence of meta-fantasies – *Blood: A Southern Fantasy* (1995), *Fabulous Harbours* (1995) and *The War Amongst the Angels: An Autobiographical Story* (1996) – brood on the real world and the multiverse through the lens of Chaos Theory: the closer you get to the world, the less you describe it. *The Metatemporal Detective* (2007) – a narrative in the Steampunk mode Moorcock had previewed as long ago as *The Warlord of the Air* (1971) and *The Land Leviathan* (1974) – continues the process, sometimes dizzyingly: as though the reader inhabited the eye of a camera increasing its focus on a closely observed reality while its bogey simultaneously wheels it backwards from the desired rapport: an old Kurasawa trick here amplified into a tool of conspectus, fantasy eyed and (once again) rejourneyed, this time through the lens of SF.

We reach the second decade of the twenty-first century, time still to make things new, but also time to sort. There are dozens of titles in *The Michael Moorcock Collection* that have not been listed in this short space, much less trawled for tidbits. The various avatars of the Eternal Champion – Elric, Kane of Old Mars, Hawkmoon, Count Brass, Corum, Von Bek – differ vastly from one another. Hawkmoon is a bit of a berk; Corum is a steely solitary at the End of Time: the joys and doleurs of the interplays amongst them can only be experienced through immersion. And the Dancers at the End of Time books, and the Nomad of the Time Stream books, and the Karl Glogauer books, and all the others. They are here now, a 100 books that make up one book. They have been fixed for reading. It is time to enter the multiverse and see the world.

September 2012

Introduction to
The Michael Moorcock Collection

Michael Moorcock

B Y 1964, AFTER I had been editing NEW WORLDS for some months and had published several science fiction and fantasy novels, including *Stormbringer*, I realised that my run as a writer was over. About the only new ideas I'd come up with were miniature computers, the multiverse and black holes, all very crudely realised, in *The Sundered Worlds*. No doubt I would have to return to journalism, writing features and editing. 'My career,' I told my friend J.G. Ballard, 'is finished.' He sympathised and told me he only had a few SF stories left in him, then he, too, wasn't sure what he'd do.

In January 1965, living in Colville Terrace, Notting Hill, then an infamous slum, best known for its race riots, I sat down at the typewriter in our kitchen-cum-bathroom and began a locally based book, designed to be accompanied by music and graphics. *The Final Programme* featured a character based on a young man I'd seen around the area and whom I named after a local greengrocer, Jerry Cornelius, 'Messiah to the Age of Science'. Jerry was as much a technique as a character. Not the 'spy' some critics described him as but an urban adventurer as interested in his psychic environment as the contemporary physical world. My influences were English and French absurdists, American noir novels. My inspiration was William Burroughs with whom I'd recently begun a correspondence. I also borrowed a few SF ideas, though I was adamant that I was not writing in any established genre. I felt I had at last found my own authentic voice.

I had already written a short novel, *The Golden Barge*, set in a nowhere, no-time world very much influenced by Peake and the surrealists, which I had not attempted to publish. An earlier auto-biographical novel, *The Hungry Dreamers*, set in Soho, was eaten by rats in a Ladbroke Grove basement. I remained unsatisfied with my style and my technique. *The Final Programme* took nine days to complete (by 20 January, 1965) with my baby daughters sometimes cradled with their bottles while I typed on. This, I should say, is my memory of events; my then wife scoffed at this story when I recounted it. Whatever the truth, the fact is I only believed I might be a serious writer after I had finished that novel, with all its flaws. But Jerry Cornelius, probably my most successful sustained attempt at unconventional fiction, was born then and ever since has remained a useful means of telling complex stories. Associated with the 60s and 70s, he has been equally at home in all the following decades. Through novels and novellas I developed a means of carrying several narratives and viewpoints on what appeared to be a very light (but tight) structure which dispensed with some of the earlier methods of fiction. In the sense that it took for granted the understanding that the novel is among other things an internal dialogue and I did not feel the need to repeat by now commonly understood modernist conventions, this fiction was post-modern.

Not all my fiction looked for new forms for the new century. Like many 'revolutionaries' I looked back as well as forward. As George Meredith looked to the eighteenth century for inspiration for his experiments with narrative, I looked to Meredith, popular Edwardian realists like Pett Ridge and Zangwill and the writers of the *fin de siècle* for methods and inspiration. An almost obsessive interest in the Fabians, several of whom believed in the possibility of benign imperialism, ultimately led to my Bastable books which examined our enduring British notion that an empire could be essentially a force for good. The first was *The Warlord of the Air*.

I also wrote my *Dancers at the End of Time* stories and novels under the influence of Edwardian humourists and absurdists like Jerome or Firbank. Together with more conventional generic books like *The Ice Schooner* or *The Black Corridor*, most of that work was done in the 1960s and 70s when I wrote the Eternal Champion supernatural adventure novels which helped support my own and others' experiments via NEW WORLDS, allowing me also to keep a family while writing books in which action and fantastic invention were paramount. Though I did them quickly, I didn't write them cynically. I have always believed, somewhat puritanically, in giving the audience good value for money. I enjoyed writing them, tried to avoid repetition, and through each new one was able to develop a few more ideas. They also continued to teach me how to express myself through image and metaphor. My Everyman became the Eternal Champion, his dreams and ambitions represented by the multiverse. He could be an ordinary person struggling with familiar problems in a contemporary setting or he could be a swordsman fighting monsters on a far-away world.

Long before I wrote *Gloriana* (in four parts reflecting the seasons) I had learned to think in images and symbols through reading John Bunyan's *Pilgrim's Progress*, Milton and others, understanding early on that the visual could be the most important part of a book and was often in itself a story as, for instance, a famous personality could also, through everything associated with their name, function as narrative. I wanted to find ways of carrying as many stories as possible in one. From the cinema I also learned how to use images as connecting themes. Images, colours, music, and even popular magazine headlines can all add coherence to an apparently random story, underpinning it and giving the reader a sense of internal logic and a satisfactory resolution, dispensing with certain familiar literary conventions.

When the story required it, I also began writing neo-realist fiction exploring the interface of character and environment, especially the city, especially London. In some books I condensed, manipulated and randomised time to achieve what I wanted, but in others the sense of 'real time' as we all generally perceive it was more suitable and could best be achieved by traditional nineteenth-century means. For the Pyat books I first looked back to the great German classic, Grimmelshausen's *Simplicissimus* and other early picaresques. I then examined the roots of a certain kind of moral fiction from Defoe through Thackeray and Meredith then to modern times where the picaresque (or rogue tale) can take the form of a road movie, for instance. While it's probably fair to say that Pyat and *Byzantium Endures* precipitated the end of my second marriage (echoed to a degree in *The Brothel in Rosenstrasse*), the late 70s and the 80s were exhilarating times for me, with *Mother London* being perhaps my own favourite novel of that period. I wanted to write something celebratory.

By the 90s I was again attempting to unite several kinds of fiction in one novel with my Second Ether trilogy. With Mandelbrot, Chaos Theory and String Theory I felt, as I said at the time, as if I were being offered a chart of my own brain. That chart made it easier for me to develop the notion of the multiverse as representing both the internal and the external, as a metaphor and as a means of structuring and rationalising an outrageously inventive and quasi-realistic narrative. The worlds of the multiverse move up and down scales or 'planes' explained in terms of mass, allowing entire universes to exist in the 'same' space. The result of developing this idea was the *War Amongst the Angels* sequence which added absurdist elements also functioning as a kind of mythology and folklore for a world beginning to understand itself in terms of new metaphysics and theoretical physics. As the cosmos becomes denser and almost infinite before our eyes, with black holes and dark matter affecting our own reality, we can explore them and observe them as our ancestors explored our planet and observed the heavens.

At the end of the 90s I'd returned to realism, sometimes with a dash of fantasy, with *King of the City* and the stories collected in *London Bone*. I also wrote a new Elric/Eternal Champion sequence, beginning with *Daughter of Dreams*, which brought the fantasy worlds of Hawkmoon, Bastable and Co. in line with my realistic and autobiographical stories, another attempt to unify all my fiction, and also offer a way in which disparate genres could be reunited, through notions developed from the multiverse and the Eternal Champion, as one giant novel. At the time I was finishing the Pyat sequence which attempted to look at the roots of the Nazi Holocaust in our European, Middle Eastern and American cultures and to ground my strange survival guilt while at the same time examining my own cultural roots in the light of an enduring anti-Semitism.

By the 2000s I was exploring various conventional ways of story-telling in the last parts of *The Metatemporal Detective* and through other homages, comics, parodies and games. I also looked back at my earliest influences. I had reached retirement age and felt like a rest. I wrote a 'prequel' to the Elric series as a graphic novel with Walter Simonson, *The Making of a Sorcerer*, and did a little online editing with FANTASTIC METROPOLIS.

By 2010 I had written a novel featuring Doctor Who, *The Coming of the Terraphiles*, with a nod to P.G. Wodehouse (a boyhood favourite), continued to write short stories and novellas and to work on the beginning of a new sequence combining pure fantasy and straight autobiography called *The Whispering Swarm* while still writing more Cornelius stories trying to unite all the various genres and sub-genres into which contemporary fiction has fallen.

Throughout my career critics have announced that I'm 'abandoning' fantasy and concentrating on literary fiction. The truth is, however, that all my life, since I became a professional writer and editor at the age of 16, I've written in whatever mode suits a story best and where necessary created a new form if an old one didn't work for me. Certain ideas are best carried on a Jerry Cornelius story, others work better as realism and others as fantasy or science fiction. Some work best as a combination. I'm sure I'll write whatever I like and will continue to experiment with all the ways there are of telling stories and carrying as many themes as possible. Whether I write about a widow coping with loneliness in her cottage or a massive, universe-size sentient spaceship searching for her children, I'll no doubt die trying to tell them all. I hope you'll find at least some of them to your taste.

One thing a reader can be sure of about these new editions is that they would not have been possible without the tremendous and indispensable help of my old friend and bibliographer John Davey. John has ensured that these Gollancz editions are definitive. I am indebted to John for many things, including his work at

Moorcock's Miscellany, my website, but his work on this edition has been outstanding. As well as being an accomplished novelist in his own right John is an astonishingly good editor who has worked with Gollancz and myself to point out every error and flaw in all previous editions, some of them not corrected since their first publication, and has enabled me to correct or revise them. I couldn't have completed this project without him. Together, I think, Gollancz, John Davey and myself have produced what will be the best editions possible and I am very grateful to him, to Malcolm Edwards, Darren Nash and Marcus Gipps for all the considerable hard work they have done to make this edition what it is.

Michael Moorcock

For Tom Disch

Part One

Part One

Chapter One

T HE TIME MACHINE is a sphere full of milky fluid in which the traveller floats enclosed in a rubber suit, breathing through a mask attached to a hose leading into the wall of the machine.

The sphere cracks as it lands and the spilled fluid is soaked up by dust. The sphere begins to roll, bumping over barren soil and rocks.

Oh, Jesus! Oh, God!
Oh, Jesus! Oh, God!
Oh, Jesus! Oh, God!
Oh, Jesus! Oh, God!
Christ! What's happening to me?
I'm fucked. I'm finished.
The bloody thing doesn't work.
Oh, Jesus! Oh, God! When will the bastard stop thumping!

Karl Glogauer curls himself into a ball as the level of the liquid falls and he sinks to the yielding plastic of the machine's inner lining.

The instruments, cryptographic, unconventional, make no sound, do not move. The sphere stops, shifts and rolls again as the last of the liquid drips from the wide split in its side.

Why did I do it? Why did I do it? Why did I do it? Why did I do it? Why did I do it? Why did I do it?

Rapidly Glogauer's eyes open and close, then his mouth stretches in a kind of yawn and his tongue flutters and he utters a groan that turns into an ululation.

He hears the ululation and thinks absently: The Voice of Tongues, the language of the unconscious... But he cannot hear what he is saying.

Air hisses and the plastic lining begins to sink, until Glogauer lies on his back against the metal of the wall. He stops crying out and looks at the jagged crack in the sphere; he has no curiosity concerning what is beyond it. He tries to move his body, but it is completely numb. He shivers as he feels the cold air that blows through the ruptured wall of the time machine. It seems to be night.

His passage through time has been difficult. Even the thick fluid has not wholly protected him, though it has doubtless saved his life. Some ribs are probably broken.

Pain comes with this idea and he discovers that he can, in fact, straighten his arms and legs.

He begins to crawl over the slippery surface towards the crack. He gasps, pauses, then moves on.

He faints, and when he recovers the air is warmer. Through the crack he can see harsh sunlight, a sky of shimmering steel. He pulls himself halfway through the crack, closing his eyes as the full strength of the sunlight strikes them. He loses consciousness again.

Christmas term, 1949
He was nine years old, born two years after his father had reached England from Austria.

On the grey gravel of the school playground the other children were screaming with laughter; they were playing a game. At the edges of the playground there were still little heaps of dirty ice. Beyond the fence the grimy South London buildings were black against the cold winter sky.

The game had begun earnestly enough and somewhat nervously Karl had suggested the rôle he play. At first he had relished the attention, but now he was crying.

'Let me down! Please, Mervyn, stop it!'

They had tied him with his arms spreadeagled against the wire netting of the playground fence. The fence bulged outwards under his weight and one of the posts threatened to come loose. He tried to free his feet.

'*Let me down!*'

Mervyn Williams, the red-faced boy who had proposed the game, began to shake the post so that Karl was swung heavily back and forth on the netting.

'Stop it! Somebody help me!'

They laughed again and he realised his cries only encouraged them, so he clenched his teeth. Tears fell down his face and he was full of a sense of bewilderment and betrayal. He had thought all of them were his friends; he had helped some of them with their work, bought others sweets, sympathised with some of them when they had been unhappy. He had thought they liked him, admired him. Why had they turned against him – even Molly, who had confided her secrets in him?

'*Please!*' he screamed. 'This wasn't in the game!'

'It is now!' laughed Mervyn Williams, his eyes bright and his face flushed as he shook the post harder.

For a few more moments Karl endured the shaking and then, instinctively, he slumped, pretending unconsciousness. He had done much the same thing before, to blackmail his mother from whom he had learnt the trick.

The school ties they had used as bonds cut into his wrists. He heard the children's voices drop.

'Is he all right?' whispered Molly Turner. 'He's not dead, is he…?'

'Don't be silly,' Williams replied uncertainly. 'He's only kidding.'

'We'd better get him down, anyway.' It was Ian Thompson's voice. 'We'll get into awful trouble if…'

He felt them untying him, their fingers fumbling with the knots.

'I can't get this one undone…'

'Here's my penknife – cut it…'

'I can't – it's my tie – my dad'll…'

'Hurry up, Brian!'

Deliberately, hanging by the single tie, he let himself sag, still keeping his eyes tightly shut.

'Give it to me. I'll cut it!'

As the last tie gave way, he fell to his knees, grazing them on the gravel, and dropped face down to the ground.

'Blimey, he really is…'

'Don't be a fool – he's still breathing. He's just fainted.'

Distantly, for he was half-convinced by his own deception, he heard their worried voices.

Williams shook him.

'Wake up, Karl. Stop mucking about.'

'I'm going to fetch Mr Matson,' said Molly Turner.

'No, don't…'

'It's a lousy game, anyway.'

'Come back, Molly!'

Most of his attention was now on the chips of gravel that dug into the left side of his face. It was easy to keep his eyes closed and ignore their hands on his body. Gradually he lost his sense of time until he heard Mr Matson's voice, deep, sardonic and unruffled as usual, over the general babble. There was silence.

'What on earth were you doing this time, Williams?'

'Nothing, sir. It was a game. It was partly Karl's idea.'

Heavy masculine hands turned him over. He was still able to keep his eyes shut.

'It was a play, sir,' said Ian Thompson, 'about Jesus. Karl was being Jesus. We've played it before, sir. We tied him to the fence. It was his idea, sir.'

'A bit unseasonable,' Mr Matson murmured, and sighed, feeling Karl's forehead.

'It was only a game, sir,' Mervyn Williams said again.

Mr Matson was taking his pulse. 'You should have known better, Williams. Glogauer isn't a strong boy.'

'I'm sorry, sir.'

'A really foolish thing to do.'

'I am sorry, sir.' Williams was almost in tears now.

'I'll take him along to Matron. I hope for your sake, Williams, that there's nothing seriously wrong with him. You'd better come and see me in the common room after school.'

Karl felt Mr Matson lift him up.

He was satisfied.

He was being carried along.

His head and side were so painful that he felt like vomiting. He had had no chance to discover where exactly the time machine had brought him, but, turning his head and opening his eyes, he saw from the dirty sheepskin jerkin and cotton loincloth of the man on his right that he was almost certainly in the Middle East.

He had meant to land in the year AD 29 in the wilderness beyond Jerusalem, near Bethlehem. He wondered if they were taking him to Jerusalem now?

He was probably in the past, for the stretcher on which they carried him was evidently made of animal skins that had not been too well cured. But perhaps not, he thought, for he had spent enough time amongst the small tribal communities of the Middle East to know that there were still people who had hardly changed their living customs since the time of Mohammed. He hoped he had not got the cracked ribs for nothing.

Two men carried the stretcher on their shoulders while others walked beside him on either side. They were all bearded and dark-skinned and wore sandals. Most of them carried staffs. There was a smell of sweat and animal fat and a musty odour he could not identify. They were walking towards a line of hills in the distance and had not noticed his awakening.

The sun was not as strong as when he had first crawled from the time machine. It was probably evening. The surrounding ground was rocky and barren and even the hills ahead seemed grey.

He winced as the stretcher lurched, moaned as the pain in his side once again became sickeningly intense. For the second time he passed out.

Our Father which art in heaven…

He had been brought up, like most of his schoolfellows, paying a certain lip service to the Christian religion. Prayers in the mornings at school. He had taken to saying two prayers at night. One was the Lord's Prayer and the other went God bless Mummy, God bless Daddy, God bless my sisters and brothers and all the dear people that surround me, and God bless me. Amen. That had been taught to him by a woman who looked after him for a while when his mother was at work. He had added to this a list of 'thank-yous' ('Thank you for a lovely day, thank you for getting the history questions right…') and 'sorrys' ('Sorry I was rude to Molly Turner, sorry I didn't own up to Mr Matson…'). He had been seventeen years old before he had been able to get to sleep without saying the ritual prayers and even then it had been his impatience to masturbate that had finally broken the habit.

Our Father which art in heaven…

His last memory of his father concerned a seaside holiday when he had been four or five. The War had been on, the trains had been crowded with soldiers, there had been many stops and changes. He remembered crossing a railway line to get to another platform, asking his father some questions about the contents of the trucks being shunted past in the sunlight. Had there been a joke? Something about giraffes?

He remembered his father as a tall, heavy man. His voice had been kind, perhaps a bit sad, and there had been a melancholy look in his eyes.

He knew now that his mother and father had been breaking up at that time and his mother had allowed his father this last holiday with him. Was it in Devon or Cornwall? What he remembered of the cliffs, rocks and beaches seemed to correspond with scenes of the West Country he had seen on television since.

He had played in an orchard that had been full of cats and a broken-down Ford in which weeds had grown. The farmhouse they had stayed in was also crammed with cats; seas of cats that had covered chairs and tables and dressers.

There had been barbed wire on the beaches, but he had not realised it spoiled the scenery. There were bridges and statues of sandstone carved by the wind and the sea. There were mysterious caves from which water ran.

It was almost the earliest, and certainly the happiest, memory of his childhood.

He never saw his father again.

God bless Mummy, God bless Daddy...

It was silly. He didn't have a daddy, didn't have any brothers and sisters.

The old woman had explained that his daddy was somewhere and that everyone was a brother or a sister.

He had accepted it.

Lonely, he thought. I am lonely. And he woke up briefly thinking he was in the indoor Anderson shelter with its sheets of reddish steel and its wire grating sides, thinking there was an air raid on. He had loved the security of the Anderson. It had been fun getting into it.

But the voices were speaking a foreign language. It was probably night, for it seemed very dark. They were no longer moving. He felt hot. There was straw beneath him. He touched the straw and, without knowing why, felt relieved. He slept.

Screaming. Tension.

His mother was shouting at Mr George upstairs. Mr George and his wife rented the two back rooms of the house.

He called up the stairs to his mother.

'Mummy! Mummy!'

Her hysterical voice: 'What is it?'

'I want to see you!'

He wanted her to stop.

'What is it, Karl? You've woken the child up now!'

She appeared on the landing above him, leaning dramatically on the banister, pulling her dressing gown about her.

'Mummy. What's the matter?'

She paused for a moment as if in decision, then collapsed slowly down the stairs. She lay at the foot now, on the dark, threadbare carpet. He sobbed and tugged at her shoulders but she was too heavy for him to move. He was panic-stricken. 'Oh, Mummy!'

Mr George came heavily down the stairs. He had a resigned expression. 'Oh, hell,' he said. 'Greta!'

Karl glared at him.

Mr George looked back at Karl and shook his head. 'She's all right, son. Come on, Greta, wake up!'

Karl stood between Mr George and his mother. Mr George shrugged and pushed him aside, then bent and pulled Karl's mother to her feet. Her long, black hair was all over her beautiful, harassed face. She opened her eyes and even Karl was surprised that she had woken up so soon.

'Where am I?' she said.

'Come off it, Greta. You're all right.'

Mr George began to lead her back upstairs.

'What about Karl?' she said.

'Don't worry about him.'

They disappeared.

The house was silent now. Karl went into the kitchen. There was an ironing board set up with an iron on it. Something was cooking on the stove. It didn't smell very nice. It was probably something Mrs George was cooking.

He heard someone descending the stairs and he ran through the kitchen into the garden.

He was crying. He was seven.

Chapter Two

In those days came John the Baptist, preaching in the wilderness of Judaea, And saying, Repent ye: for the kingdom of heaven is at hand. For this is he that was spoken of by the prophet Esaias, saying, The voice of one crying in the wilderness, Prepare ye the way of the Lord, make his paths straight. And the same John had his raiment of camel's hair, and a leathern girdle about his loins; and his meat was locusts and wild honey. Then went out to him Jerusalem, and all Judaea, and all the region round about Jordan, And were baptised of him in Jordan, confessing their sins.

(Matthew 3: 1–6)

T HEY WERE WASHING him.

He felt the cold water running over his body and he gasped. They had stripped off his protective suit and there were now thick layers of sheepskin against his ribs, bound to him by bands of leather.

There was less pain, but he felt very weak and hot. The mental confusion of the weeks preceding his entering the time machine, the journey itself and now the fever made it difficult for him to begin to understand what was happening to him. Everything had had, for so long, the quality of a dream. He still could not really believe in the time machine. Perhaps he was just high on something? His hold on reality had never been particularly strong; through most of his adolescence and adult life only certain instincts had enabled him to preserve his physical well-being. Yet the water pouring over him, the touch of the sheepskin round his ribs, the straw beneath him, all had a sharper reality in their way than anything he had known since he was a child.

*

11

He was in a building – or perhaps a cave, it was too gloomy to tell – and the straw had been saturated by the water.

Two men in sandals and loincloths sluiced water down on him from their earthenware jars. One wore a length of cotton pushed back over his shoulders. They both had swarthy Semitic features, large dark eyes and full beards. Their faces were expressionless, even when they paused as he looked up at them. For several moments they stared back, holding their water jars to their hairy chests.

Glogauer's knowledge of ancient written Aramaic was good, but he was not sure of his ability to speak the language in order to make himself understood. He would try English first since it would be ridiculous if he had not moved through time and he tried to speak an archaic tongue to modern Israelis or Arabs.

He said weakly: 'Do you speak English?'

One of the men frowned and the other, with the cotton cloak, began to smile, speaking a few words to his companion and laughing. The other answered in a graver tone.

Glogauer thought he recognised a few words and he began to grin himself. It was ancient Aramaic they were speaking. He was sure of it. He wondered if he could phrase a sentence they might understand.

He cleared his throat. He wet his lips. 'Where – be – this place?' he asked thickly.

Now they both frowned, shaking their heads and lowering their water jars to the ground.

Feeling his energy begin to dissipate, Glogauer said urgently, 'I – seek – a Nazarene – Jesus…'

'Nazarene. Jesus.' The taller of the two repeated the words but they did not seem to mean anything to him. He shrugged.

The other, however, only repeated the word Nazarene, uttering it slowly as if it had some special significance for him. He muttered a few words to the other man, then moved away, out of Glogauer's field of vision.

Glogauer tried to sit up and gesture to the remaining man, who looked at him with brooding puzzlement.

'What – year,' Glogauer said slowly, 'doth – the Roman emperor – sit in – Rome?'

It was a confusing question to ask, he realised. Christ had been crucified in the fifteenth year of Tiberius's reign, and that was why he had asked the question. He tried to phrase it better.

'How many – year – doth Tiberius rule?'

'Tiberius!' The man frowned.

Glogauer's ear was adjusting to the accent now and he tried to imitate it better. 'Tiberius. The emperor of the Romans. How many years has he ruled?'

'How many?' The man shook his head. 'I know not.'

At least, thought Glogauer, he had been able to make himself understood. His six months in the British Museum studying Aramaic had been useful, after all. This language was different – perhaps two thousand years earlier – and had closer affinities with Hebrew, but it had been surprisingly easy to communicate with the man. He remembered how strange it had seemed when he had had none of his usual difficulties when learning this particular language. One or two of his crankier friends had suggested that it was his race memory that served him. At times, he had been almost convinced by the explanation.

'Where is this place?' he asked.

The man looked surprised. 'Why, it is the wilderness,' he said. 'The wilderness beyond Machaerus. Know you not that?'

In biblical times Machaerus had been a large town lying to the south-east of Jerusalem, on the other side of the Dead Sea. It had been built on the flanks of a mountain, guarded by a magnificent palace-fortress constructed by Herod Antipas. Again Glogauer felt his spirits rise. In the twentieth century few would have known the name of Machaerus, let alone used it as a reference point.

There was almost no doubt at all that he was in the past and that the period was some time in the reign of Tiberius, unless the man he spoke to was completely ignorant and had no idea who Tiberius was.

But had he missed the crucifixion? Had he come at the wrong time?

If so, what was he to do now? For his time machine was wrecked, was perhaps beyond repair.

He let himself sink back onto the straw and closed his eyes, and a familiar sense of depression once again completely filled him.

The first time he had tried to commit suicide he had been fifteen. He had tied string round a hook halfway up the wall in the locker room at school. He had placed the noose around his neck and jumped off the bench.

The hook had been torn away from the wall, bringing with it a shower of plaster. His neck had felt sore for the rest of the day.

The other man was now returning, bringing someone else with him.

The sound of their sandals on the stone seemed very loud to Glogauer.

He looked up at the newcomer.

He was a giant and he moved like a cat through the gloom. His eyes were large, piercing and brown. His skin was burned dark and his hairy arms were heavily muscled. A goatskin covered his great barrel chest and reached to below his thighs. In his right hand he carried a thick staff. His black, curly hair hung around his head and face; his red lips could be seen beneath the bushy beard that covered the upper part of his chest.

He seemed tired.

He leaned on his staff and looked reflectively at Glogauer.

Glogauer stared back at him, astonished at the impression he had of the man's tremendous physical presence.

When the newcomer spoke, it was in a deep voice, but too rapidly for Glogauer to follow. He shook his head.

'Speak – more slowly…' he said.

The big man squatted down beside him.

'Who art thou?'

Glogauer hesitated. Obviously he could not tell the man the truth. He had, in fact, already invented what seemed to him a plausible story, but he had not planned to be found in this way and the original story would not do. He had hoped to land unseen and disguise himself as a traveller from Syria, counting on the chance that the local accents would be different enough to explain his own unfamiliarity with the language.

'From where do you come?' asked the man patiently.

Glogauer answered cautiously.

'I am from the north.'

'The north. Not from Egypt?' He looked at Glogauer expectantly, almost hopefully. Glogauer decided that if he sounded as if he came from Egypt, then it would be best to agree with the man, adding his own embellishment in order to avoid any future complications.

'I came out of Egypt two years since,' he said.

The big man nodded, apparently satisfied. 'So you are from Egypt. That is what we thought. And evidently you are a magus with your strange clothes and your chariot of iron drawn by spirits. Good. Your name is Jesus, I am told, and you are the Nazarene.'

Evidently the man must have mistaken Glogauer's enquiry as a statement of his own name. He smiled and shook his head.

'I seek Jesus, the Nazarene,' he said.

The man seemed disappointed. 'Then, what is your name?'

Glogauer had also considered this. He knew his own name would seem too outlandish to the people of biblical times and so he had decided to use his father's first name.

'My name is Emmanuel,' he told the man.

'Emmanuel...' He nodded, seeming satisfied. He rubbed his lips with the tip of his little finger and stared contemplatively at the ground. 'Emmanuel... yes...'

Glogauer was puzzled. It seemed to him that he had been mistaken for someone else that the big man had been expecting, that he had given answers that satisfied the man that he, Glogauer, was the man for whom he waited. He wondered now if the choice of name had been wise in the circumstances, for Emmanuel meant in Hebrew 'God with us' and almost certainly had a mystic significance for his questioner.

Glogauer began to feel uncomfortable. There were things he had to establish for himself, questions of his own to ask, and he did not like his present position. Until he was in better physical condition, he could not leave here, could not afford to anger his interrogator. At least, he thought, they were not antagonistic. But what did they expect of him?

'You must try to concentrate on your work, Glogauer.'

'You're too dreamy, Glogauer. Your head's always in the clouds. Now...'

'You'll stay behind after school, Glogauer...'

'Why did you try to run away, Glogauer? Why aren't you happy here?'

'Really, you must meet me halfway if we're going to...'

'I think I shall have to ask your mother to take you away from the school...'

'Perhaps you are trying – but you must try harder. I expected a great deal of you, Glogauer, when you first came here. Last term you were doing wonderfully, and now...'

'How many schools were you at before you came here? Good heavens!'

'It's my belief that you were led into this, Glogauer, so I shan't be too hard on you this time...'

'Don't look so miserable, son – you can do it.'

'Listen to me, Glogauer. Pay attention, for heaven's sake...'

'You've got the brains, young man, but you don't seem to have the application...'

'Sorry? It's not good enough to be sorry. You must listen...'

'We expect you to try much harder next term.'

'And what is your name?' Glogauer asked the squatting man.

He straightened up, looking broodingly down on Glogauer.

'You do not know me?'

Glogauer shook his head.

'You have not heard of John, called the Baptist?'

Glogauer tried to hide his surprise, but evidently John the

Baptist saw that his name was familiar. He nodded his shaggy head.

'You do know of me, I see.'

A sense of relief swept through him then. According to the New Testament, the Baptist had been killed some time before Christ's crucifixion. It was strange, however, that John of all people had not heard of Jesus of Nazareth. Did that mean, after all, that Christ had not existed?

The Baptist combed at his beard with his fingers. 'Well, magus, now I must decide, eh?'

Glogauer, concerned with his own thoughts, looked up at him absently. 'What must you decide?'

'If you be the friend of the prophecies or the false one we have been warned against by Adonai.'

Glogauer became nervous. 'I have made no claims. I am merely a stranger, a traveller…'

The Baptist laughed. 'Aye – a traveller in a magic chariot. My brothers tell me they saw it arrive. There was a sound like thunder, a flash like lightning – and all at once your chariot was there, rolling across the wilderness. They have seen many wonders, my brothers, but none so marvellous as the appearance of your chariot.'

'The chariot is not magic,' Glogauer said hastily, realising that what he said could hardly be understood by the Baptist. 'It is – a kind of engine – the Romans have such things. You must have heard of them. They are made by ordinary men, not sorcerers…'

The Baptist nodded his head slowly. 'Aye – like the Romans. The Romans would deliver me into the hands of my enemies, the children of Herod.'

Although he knew a great deal about the politics of the period, Glogauer said: 'Why is that?'

'You must know why. Do I not speak against the Romans who enslave Judaea? Do I not speak against the unlawful things that Herod does? Do I not prophesy the time when all those who are not righteous shall be destroyed and Adonai's kingdom will be restored on Earth as the old prophets said it would be? I say to the people "Be ready for that day when ye shall take up the sword to do Adonai's will".' The unrighteous know that they will perish on this day, and they would destroy me.'

Although John's words were fiery, his tone was perfectly matter-of-fact. There was no hint of insanity or even fanaticism in his face or bearing. Karl was reminded of an Anglican vicar reading a familiar sermon whose meaning for him had long since lost its edge.

'You are arousing the people to rid the land of the Romans, is that it?' Karl asked.

'Aye – the Romans and their creature Herod.'

'And who would you put in their place?'

'The rightful king of Judaea.'

'And who is that?'

John frowned and gave him a peculiar, sidelong look. 'Adonai will tell us. He will give us a sign when the rightful king comes.'

'Do you know what the sign will be?'

'I will know when it comes.'

'There are prophecies, then?'

'Aye, there are prophecies…'

The attribution of this revolutionary plan to Adonai (one of the spoken names of Jahweh and meaning The Lord) seemed to Glogauer merely a means of giving it extra weight. In a world where politics and religion, even in the West, were inextricably bound together, it was necessary to ascribe a supernatural origin to the plan.

Indeed, Glogauer thought, it was more than likely that John really did believe his idea had been directly inspired by God, for the Greeks on the other side of the Mediterranean had not yet stopped arguing about the origins of inspiration – whether it originated in man or was placed there by the gods.

That John accepted him as an Egyptian magician of some kind did not particularly surprise Glogauer, either. The circumstances of his arrival must have seemed extraordinarily miraculous and at the same time acceptable, particularly to a people who eagerly wished confirmation of their beliefs in such things.

John turned towards the entrance. 'I must meditate,' he said. 'I must pray. You will remain here until guidance is sent to me.'

He strode rapidly away.

Glogauer sank back on the wet straw. Somehow his appearance was bound up with John's beliefs – or at least the Baptist was attempting to reconcile that appearance with his beliefs, interpret his arrival, perhaps, in terms of biblical prophecies and so forth. Glogauer felt helpless. How would the Baptist use him? Would he decide, finally, that he was some kind of malign creature and kill him? Or would he decide that he was a prophet of some description and demand prophecies he would not be able to give?

Glogauer sighed and reached out weakly to touch the far wall.

It was limestone. He was in a limestone cave. Caves suggested that John and his men were probably in hiding – already sought as bandits by the Romans and Herodian soldiers. This meant that he was also in ordinary physical danger if the soldiers should discover John's hideout.

The atmosphere in the cave was surprisingly humid.

It must be very hot outside.

He felt drowsy.

The summer camp, Isle of Wight, 1950
The first night he was there an urn of scalding tea had been overturned on his right thigh. It had been horribly painful, blistering almost at once.

'Be a man, Glogauer!' said a red-faced Mr Patrick, the master in charge of the camp. 'Be a man!'

He tried not to cry as they clumsily stretched plaster over the cotton-wool.

His sleeping bag was right beside an anthill. He lay in it while the other children played.

The next day Mr Patrick told the children that they had to 'earn' the pocket-money the parents had given him for safe-keeping.

'We'll see which of you children have guts and which haven't,' said Mr Patrick, swishing the cane through the air as he stood in the clearing around which the tents were grouped. The children stood in two long lines – one for the girls, one for the boys.

'Get in line, Glogauer!' called Mr Patrick. 'Threepence a stroke on the hand – sixpence a stroke on the bottom. Don't be cowardly, Glogauer!'

Reluctantly, Glogauer joined the line.

The cane rose and fell. Mr Patrick breathed heavily.

'Six strokes on the bottom – that's three shillings.' He handed the money to the little girl.

More strokes, more money paid out.

Karl became nervous as his turn came closer.

Finally he broke out of line and walked away towards the tents.

'Glogauer! Where's your spirit, boy? Don't you want any pocket-money?' came Mr Patrick's coarse, bantering voice behind him.

Glogauer shook his head, beginning to cry.

Glogauer entered his tent and threw himself on his sleeping bag, sobbing.

Mr Patrick's voice could still be heard outside.

'Be a man, Glogauer! Be a man, boy!'

Karl began to take out his writing-paper and ballpoint pen. His tears fell on the paper as he wrote the letter home to his mother.

Outside he could hear the sound of the cane smacking against the children's flesh.

The pain in his thigh got worse during the next day and he was generally ignored by the masters and the children. Even the woman who was supposed to be 'matron' (Patrick's wife) told him to look after himself, that the scald was nothing.

The following two days, before his mother arrived to collect him from the camp, were the most miserable he had ever suffered.

Shortly before his mother's arrival, Mrs Patrick made an attempt to cut off the blisters with a pair of nail scissors so that they wouldn't look too bad.

His mother took him away and later wrote to Mr Patrick asking for her money back, saying that it was disgusting the way he ran his camp.

He wrote back saying that he would not return the money and that if she asked him, madam, she had a weakling for a son. If you want my opinion, he said in the letter that Karl read when he got the chance, your son's a bit of a pansy.

A few years later, Mr Patrick, his wife and staff, were prosecuted and sent to prison for their various acts of sadism during the summer camps they ran on the Isle of Wight.

Chapter Three

I N THE MORNINGS, and sometimes in the evenings, they would pick him up on his stretcher and take him outside.

This was not, as he had first suspected, a transitory bandit camp, but an established community. There were fields irrigated by a nearby spring in which they grew corn; flocks of goats and sheep which were pastured in the hills.

Their life was quiet and leisurely, and for the most part they ignored Glogauer as they went about their daily business.

Sometimes the Baptist would appear and ask after his health. More rarely he would ask some cryptic question which Glogauer would answer as best he could.

They seemed a gentle people, given to considerably more minor religious rites than Glogauer would have thought normal for even such a community as this. At least, he gathered that they were religious rites that they were called to so frequently, for they were conducted where he could not see them.

Glogauer was left chiefly with his own thoughts, his memories and his speculations. His ribs healed very slowly and he began to fret, wondering if he would ever achieve the goal he had come here for.

Glogauer was surprised at how few women there were in the community. The atmosphere was almost that of a monastery and most of the men avoided the women. He began to realise that this was probably very much a religious community. Perhaps these people were Essenes?

If they were Essenes it would explain a number of things about them – absence, in the main, of women (few Essenes believed in marriage), John's particular apocalyptic beliefs, the preponderance of religious observances, the rigidly simple life these people led, the fact that they seemed deliberately to have set themselves apart from others...

Glogauer put it to the Baptist the next chance he got.

'John – are your people called Essenes?'

The Baptist nodded.

'How did you know that?' he asked Glogauer.

'I – I had heard of you. Are you outlawed by Herod?'

John shook his head. 'Herod would outlaw us if he dared, but he has no cause. We lead our own lives, harming no-one, making no attempt to enforce our beliefs on others. From time to time I go out and preach our creed – but there is no law against that. We respect the commandments of Moses and only preach that others should obey them. We speak only for righteousness. Even Herod cannot find fault with that...'

Now Glogauer understood better the nature of some of the questions John had been asking him; understood why these people behaved and lived in the way they did.

He realised, too, how it was that they had accepted the manner of his arrival with so little fuss. A sect like the Essenes, which practised self-mortification and starvation, must be quite used to seeing visions in this hot wilderness.

He remembered, also, that he had once come across a theory that John the Baptist had been an Essene and that many of the early Christian ideas had been derived from Essene beliefs.

The Essenes, for instance, indulged in ritual bathing – baptism; they believed in a group of twelve (the apostles) who were the elect of God and would be judges on the last day; they preached a creed of 'love thy neighbour'; they believed, as the early Christians had believed, that they were living in the days immediately before Armageddon when the final battle between light and darkness, good and evil, would be fought and when all men would be brought to judgement. As with certain Christian sects, there were Essenes who believed that they represented the forces of light and that others – Herod or the Roman conquerors – represented the forces of darkness and that it was their destiny to destroy these forces. These political beliefs were inextricably bound up with the religious beliefs and although it was possible that someone like John the Baptist was cynically using the Essenes to further his own political ends, it was really quite unlikely.

In twentieth-century terms, Glogauer thought, these Essenes would be regarded as neurotics, with their almost paranoiac mysticism that led them to invent secret languages and the like – a sure indication of their mentally unbalanced condition.

All this occurred to Glogauer the psychiatrist manqué, but Glogauer the man was torn between the poles of extreme rationalism and the desire to be convinced by the mysticism itself.

The Baptist had wandered away before Glogauer could ask him any further questions. He watched the tall man as he disappeared inside a large cave, then turned his attention to the distant fields where a thin Essene guided a plough pulled by two other members of the sect.

Glogauer studied the yellow hills and the rocks. He was becoming eager to see more of this world and at the same time wondering what had become of his time machine. Was it in complete disrepair? Would he ever be able to leave this period of time and return to the twentieth century?

Sex and religion.

The church club he had joined to find friends.

A nature ramble, 1954

He and Veronica had lost the others in Farlowe's Wood.

She was fat and blowsy even at thirteen, but she was a girl.

'Let's sit here and rest,' he said, indicating a hillock in a little glade surrounded by shrubs.

They sat down together.

They said nothing.

His eyes fixed not on her round, coarse-skinned face, but on the little silver crucifix that dangled by a chain about her neck.

'We'd better start looking for the others,' she said nervously. 'They'll be worrying about us, Karl.'

'Let them find us,' he said. 'We'll soon hear them shouting.'

'They might go home.'

'They won't go without us. Don't worry. We'll hear them shouting...'

He lurched forward, reaching for her navy-blue cardigan-clad shoulders, his eyes still fixed on the crucifix.

He tried to kiss her lips but she turned her head away. 'Give us a kiss, then,' he said breathlessly. Even at that moment he realised how ludicrous he sounded, what a fool he was making of himself, but he forced himself to continue. 'Give us a kiss, Veronica...'

'No, Karl. Stop it.'

'Come on...'

She began to struggle, broke away from him and got to her feet.

He was blushing now.

'Sorry,' he said. 'Sorry.'

'All right...'

'I thought you wanted to,' he said.

'You needn't've jumped at me like that. Not very romantic.'

'Sorry...'

She began to walk away, the crucifix swinging. He was fascinated by it. Did it represent some sort of amulet to ward off the sort of danger she probably considered she'd just avoided?

He followed her.

Soon they heard the shouts of the others through the trees and Karl inexplicably felt sick.

Several of the other girls began to giggle and one of the boys leered.

'What've you been up to, then?'

'Nothing,' said Karl.

But Veronica didn't say anything. Although she hadn't been prepared to kiss him, she was obviously enjoying the insinuations.

She held his hand on the way back.

It was dark when they returned to the church and had a cup of tea. They sat together. All the time he stared at the crucifix that hung between her already large breasts.

The others had all gathered together at the other end of the bare church hall. Sometimes Karl heard one of the girls giggle and saw a boy glance in their direction. He began to feel quite pleased with himself. He moved closer to her.

'Can I get you another cup of tea, Veronica?'

She was staring at the floor. 'No, thanks. I'd better be getting back. My mum and dad'll be worrying about me.'

'I'll see you home if you like.'

She hesitated.

'It's not far out of my way,' he said.

'All right.'

They got up and he took her hand, waving to the others.

'Cheerio, everybody. See you Thursday,' he said.

The girls' laughter grew uncontrollable and he blushed again.

'Don't do anything I wouldn't do,' shouted one of the boys.

Karl winked at him.

They walked through the well-lit suburban streets, both too embarrassed to speak, her hand limp in his.

When they reached her front door she paused, then said hastily, 'I'd better be getting in.'

'Aren't you going to give me a kiss now?' he asked. He was still staring at the crucifix on her navy-blue cardigan.

She pecked hastily at his cheek.

'You can do better than that,' he said.

'I've got to be getting in now.'

'Come on,' he said, 'give us a proper kiss.' He was close to panic, blushing heavily and sweating. He reached towards her, forcing himself to hold her arms although now he was beginning to be nauseated by her fat, coarse face and heavy, lumpen body.

'No!'

The light went on behind the door and he heard her father's voice growling in the hall.

'That you, Veronica?'

He dropped his hands. 'Okay, if you're going to be like that,' he said.

'I'm sorry,' she began, 'it's just that...'

The door opened and a man in shirtsleeves stood there. He was as fat and as coarse-featured as his daughter.

''Ullo, 'ullo,' he said, 'got a boyfriend then, have you?'

'This is Karl,' she said. 'He brought me home. He's at the club.'

'You could 'ave brought her home a bit earlier, young man,' said her father. 'Want to come in for a cup of tea or something?'

'No, thanks,' said Karl. 'Got to be getting back. Cheerio, Veronica. See you Thursday.'

'Maybe,' she said.

The following Thursday he arrived at the club for the Bible discussion group. Veronica wasn't there.

'Her dad's stopped her,' one of the girls told him. 'Must've been because of you.' She spoke contemptuously and he was puzzled.

'We hardly did anything,' he said.

'That's what she said,' the girl told him, smiling. 'She said you weren't much good at it.'

'What d'you mean? She wouldn't...'

'She said you didn't know how to kiss properly.'

'She didn't give me the chance.'

'That's what she said, anyway,' said the girl and glanced at the others.

Karl knew they were baiting him, even sensed that they were, in their way, flirting with him, were intrigued with him, but he couldn't stop himself blushing and he left the discussion group early.

He never went back to the church club, but his masturbatory fantasies of the next few weeks were filled with Veronica and the little silver cross hanging between her breasts. Even when he imagined her naked, the cross remained there. It was this, in fact, that began chiefly to excite him, and long after Veronica was gone from his dreams, he would think of girls with small silver crucifixes hanging between their breasts and the thought would arouse him to incredible excesses of pleasure.

Chapter Four

In the beginning was the Word, and the Word was with God, and the Word was God. The same was in the beginning with God. All things were made by him; and without him was not any thing made that was made. In him was life; and the life was the light of men. And the light shineth in the darkness; and the darkness comprehended it not. There was a man sent from God, whose name was John. The same came for a witness, to bear witness of the Light, that all men through him might believe. He was not that Light, but was sent to bear witness of that Light. That was the true Light, which lighteth every man that cometh into the world. He was in the world, and the world was made by him, and the world knew him not. He came unto his own, and his own received him not. But as many as received him, to them gave he power to become the sons of God, even to them that believe on his name: Which were born, not of blood, not of the will of the flesh, nor of the will of man, but of God.

(John 1: 1–13)

L ONELY, LONELY, LONELY...
      Oh, Jesus...
          Stop!
               Fo-ol
STOP   Fo
          STOP   ol   NO!
    Jes...
          STOP
          I love you... STOP.
Jesus, I...   STOP
             Lonely...

Lonely...
des... need... must lo –
STOP
lonely, lonely, lonely...
Oh, lonely, lonely...

Acne. Washing. Lonely. Rationalism. Fucking a huge silver cross.

His ribs were mending.

In the evenings, now, he would limp to the entrance of his cave and listen to the chanting of the Essenes as they offered up their evening prayer. For some obscure reason, the monotonous chanting would bring tears to his eyes and he would begin to sob uncontrollably.

At this stage of his recovery, he was often filled with depressions that would make him think of suicide.

He had turned on all the gas fires in the house and had timed things to coincide with his mother's return from work.

Just before she opened the front gate and walked up the path to unlock the door, he lay down in the sitting room before the main fire.

When she had come in she had screamed, picked him up, put him on the sofa and had broken every single window in the downstairs part of the house before she thought to turn the fires off and call the doctor.

When the doctor came, she had a story for him – about an accident. But the doctor had seemed to know all about it. He had been none too sympathetic with Karl.

'You're after the limelight, young man,' he said when Karl's mother was out of the room. 'You're after the limelight, if you ask me.'

Karl had begun to cry.

'We'll go on holiday,' his mother said, when the doctor had left. 'What's the matter? Not getting on well at school? We'll go on holiday.'

'It's nothing to do with school,' he sobbed.

'Then what is it?'

'It's *you*…'

'Me? Me? Why me? What have I got to do with it? What are you trying to say?'

'Nothing.' He became sullen.

'I must phone the people to come and put the glass in,' she said, hurrying from the room. 'It'll cost a fortune.'

Love me, love me, love me…

Lonely…

Our Father which art in heaven, hallowed be thy name, thy kingdom come…

LOVE ME!

Floating, bigger than the world, little circumcised cock in hand, silver clouds shaped like great, soft crosses, drifting, drifting, coming, coming…

LOVE ME!

Bill Haley and his Comets. See ya later, alligator. And for three and a half months, God was forgotten.

For a month, John the Baptist was away and Glogauer lived with the Essenes, finding it surprisingly easy, as his health improved, to join in their daily life.

He discovered that the Essene township consisted of a sprawling mixture of single-storey houses, built of limestone and clay brick, and the caves that were to be found on both sides of the shallow valley. Some of the caves were natural, and others had been hollowed out by previous occupants of the valley and by the Essenes themselves.

The Essenes shared their goods in common and some members of this particular sect had, as Glogauer had noticed earlier, wives, though most of them led completely monastic lives.

Glogauer learned to his surprise that most of the Essenes were pacifists, refusing to own or to make weapons. Their beliefs did not quite fit in with some of the Baptist's more warlike pronouncements, yet the sect plainly tolerated and revered John.

Perhaps their hatred of the Romans overcame their principles. Perhaps they were not absolutely sure of John's intentions. Possibly he had been deliberately obscure on this point – or maybe Glogauer had failed to understand him. Whatever the reason for their toleration of him, however, there was little doubt that John the Baptist was virtually their leader.

The life of the Essenes consisted of ritual bathing three times a day, of prayer with all meals and at dawn and at dusk, and of work.

The work was not difficult.

Sometimes Glogauer guided a plough pulled by two other members of the sect; sometimes he helped pull a plough; sometimes he looked after the goats that were allowed to graze on the hillsides.

It was a peaceful, ordered life, and even the unhealthy aspects were so much a matter of routine that Glogauer hardly noticed them after a while.

Tending the goats, he would lie on the hilltop, looking out over the wilderness. The wilderness was not a desert, but rocky scrubland sufficient to feed animals like goats or sheep.

The scrubland was broken by low-lying bushes and a few small trees growing along the banks of the river that doubtless ran into the Dead Sea.

It was uneven ground. In outline it had the appearance of a stormy lake, frozen and turned yellow and brown.

Beyond the Dead Sea lay Jerusalem.

Glogauer thought often of Jerusalem.

Obviously Christ had not yet entered the city for the last time.

John the Baptist (if the New Testament could be relied upon) would have to die before that happened. Salome would have to dance for Herod and the Baptist's great head would have to be severed from its body.

Glogauer felt guilty at the way in which the thought excited him. Should he not warn the Baptist?

He knew that he would not. He had been specifically warned

before he entered the time machine that he should make no attempt to alter the course of history. He argued to himself that he had no clear idea of the course that the history of this time had taken. There were only legends, no purely historical records. The books of the New Testament had been written decades or even centuries after the events which they described. They had never been historically authenticated. Surely, then, it made no difference if he interfered with events?

But he still knew that he would make no attempt to warn John of his danger.

He realised dimly that the reason for this was because he wanted the events to be true. He wanted the New Testament to be right.

Soon he must begin to seek out Jesus.

His mother moved frequently, although she tended to remain in roughly the same area, selling a house in one part of South London and buying a house half a mile away.

After his brief phase as a rock-and-roll fan, they moved to Thornton Heath and he joined the choir of the local church. His voice was good and tuneful, and the curate who took choir practice began to show a special interest in him. Initially they discussed music, but soon their conversations would turn more and more to religion. Karl would ask the curate for advice on his rather general problems of conscience. How could he live an ordinary life of ordinary activity without hurting anyone's feelings? Why were people so violent to each other? Why were there wars?

Mr Younger's answers were just about as woolly and as general as Karl's questions, but he gave them in a deep, confident, reassuring voice that always made Karl feel better.

They went for walks together. Mr Younger would put his arm around Karl's shoulders.

One weekend the choir went to Winchester for a festival and they stayed at a youth hostel. Karl shared a room with Mr Younger.

Late at night Mr Younger crawled into Karl's bed.

'I wish you were a girl, Karl,' said Mr Younger, stroking Karl's head.

Karl was too disturbed to reply, but he responded when Mr Younger put his hand on his genitals.

They made love all that night, but in the morning Karl felt disgusted and punched Mr Younger in the chest and said that if he ever tried anything again he would tell his mother.

Mr Younger cried and said he was sorry, couldn't he and Karl continue to be friends, but Karl felt that somehow Mr Younger had betrayed him. Mr Younger said that he loved Karl – not in that way, but in a Christian way – and that he had enjoyed his company so much. But Karl wouldn't speak to him and avoided him in the coach on the way home to Thornton Heath.

Karl stayed in the choir for a few weeks more, but there was tension between him and Mr Younger.

At the end of an evening choir practice, Mr Younger asked Karl to stay behind and Karl was torn between disgust and desire.

Finally he did stay behind and let Mr Younger stroke his genitals under a poster which showed a plain wooden cross with the slogan GOD IS LOVE underneath.

Karl began to laugh hysterically and ran away from the church and never went back again.

He was fifteen.

Silver crosses equal women.

Wooden crosses equal men.

He often thought of himself as a wooden cross. He would have mild hallucinations between sleeping and waking where he was a heavy wooden cross pursuing a delicate silver cross through fields of darkness.

By seventeen he had completely lost interest in formal Christianity and became obsessed with pagan religion, particularly Celtic mysticism and Mithraism. He had had an affair with the wife of a sergeant-major who lived in Kilburn and whom he had met at a party given by a woman he had met through the correspondence columns of the short-lived magazine *Avilion*.

The wife of the sergeant-major (he was somewhere in the Far

East) had worn a small silver Celtic cross, a 'sun cross', about her neck and that was what had first attracted him. It had taken him half a bottle of gin, however, before he had dared put his arm around her thin shoulders and later, in the darkness, put his hand between her thighs and feel her cunt beneath the satinette knickers.

After Deirdre Thompson, he had success after success with the plain-faced women of the group, all of whom, he discovered, wore exactly the same kind of satinette knickers.

Within six months he was exhausted, hating the neurotic women, loathing himself, bored with Celtic mysticism. He had been living away from home most of the time, mainly at Deirdre Thompson's house, but now he went home and had a nervous breakdown.

His mother decided he needed a change and gave him the fare to visit some friends he had made in Hamburg.

His Hamburg friends believed that they were the descendants of those who had perished when Atlantis was destroyed by atom bombs dropped from flying saucers by unsympathetic spirits from Mars.

There was a succession of plain-faced German women this time. Unlike their British sisters, they all wore black nylon lace panties.

It made a change.

In Hamburg he became militantly anti-Christian, claiming that Christianity was the perversion of an older faith, a Nordic faith.

But he could never quite accept that this faith in its purest form had been the faith of Atlantis, and at last he fell out with his German friends, found the rest of Germany generally unsympathetic, and left for Tel Aviv where he knew the owner of a bookshop specialising in works of occult lore, mainly in French.

It was in Tel Aviv, in conversation with a Hungarian painter, that he learnt of Jung and dismissed him as nonsense. He became even more withdrawn and one morning took a bus into the rural near-desert. Eventually he wound up in the Anti-Lebanon where the people spoke the closest thing to ancient Aramaic he had ever heard. He found them hospitable; he enjoyed living with them. He lived with them for four months before he returned to Tel Aviv and, in a receptive frame of mind, talked about Jung again with the Hungarian. In the occult bookshop and in the other bookshops and libraries of Tel Aviv, he could discover nothing of Jung's in English. He decided to leave for England and borrowed the fare from the British consulate.

As soon as he got back to South London he went to the local library and spent a lot of time there reading Jung.

His mother asked him when he was going to get a job.

He told her that he intended to study psychology and would eventually become a psychiatrist.

The Essenes' way of life was comfortable enough, for all its simplicity.

They had given him a goatskin loincloth and a staff and, except for the fact that he was watched all the time, they appeared to have accepted him as a kind of lay member of the sect.

Sometimes they questioned him casually about his chariot – the time machine they intended soon to bring in from the desert – and he told them that it had borne him from Egypt to Syria and then to here. They accepted the miracle calmly. They were used to miracles.

The Essenes had seen stranger things than his time machine.

They had seen men walk on water and angels descend to and from heaven; they had heard the voice of God and his archangels as well as the tempting voice of Satan and his minions.

They wrote all these things down in their vellum scrolls which were merely a record of the supernatural, as their other scrolls were records of their daily lives and of the news that travelling members of their sect brought to them.

They lived constantly in the presence of God and spoke to God and were answered by God when they had sufficiently mortified their flesh and starved themselves and chanted their prayers beneath the blazing sun of Judaea.

Karl Glogauer grew his hair long and let his beard come

unchecked. His face and body were soon burned dark by the sun. He mortified his flesh and starved himself and chanted his prayers beneath the sun, as they did.

But he rarely heard God and only once thought he saw an archangel with wings of fire.

One day they took him to the river and baptised him with the name he had first given John the Baptist. They called him Emmanuel.

The ceremony, with its chanting and its swaying, was very heady and left him completely euphoric and happier than he had ever remembered.

Chapter Five

I N SPITE OF his willingness to experience the Essenes' visions,
Glogauer was disappointed.

On the other hand he was surprised that he felt so well considering all the self-inflicted hardships he had undergone. Also he
felt relaxed in the company of these strange men and women
who were, he had to admit, undoubtedly insane by any normal
standard. Perhaps it was because their insanity was not so very
different from his own that after a while he stopped wondering
about it.

Monica.

Monica had no silver cross.

They had first met when he was working at Darley Grange
Mental Hospital as a male orderly. He had thought that he would
be able to work his way up. She was a psychiatric social worker
who had seemed more sympathetic than the rest when he had
been trying to get someone to listen to him about the hardships
the patients were made to undergo, the petty torments that other
orderlies and nurses put them through, the blows, the shouts.

'We can't get the right sort of staff, you see,' she had told him.
'The money's so low...'

'Then they ought to pay more.'

Instead of shrugging, as the others did, she had nodded. 'I
know. I've written two letters to *The Guardian* about it – not sign-
ing my name, you know – and one of them was published.'

He had left shortly afterwards and didn't see her for some years.

He was twenty.

John the Baptist returned one evening, striding over the hills, followed by twenty or so of his closest disciples.

Glogauer saw him as he prepared to drive the goats into their cave for the night. He waited for John to approach him.

At first the Baptist did not recognise him and then he laughed.

'Well, Emmanuel, you have become an Essene, I see. Have they baptised you yet?'

Glogauer nodded. 'They have.'

'Good.' The Baptist frowned then, as some other thought occurred to him. 'I have been to Jerusalem,' he said. 'To see friends.'

'And what is the news from Jerusalem?'

The Baptist looked at him candidly. 'That you are probably not a spy of Herod or the Romans.'

'I am glad you have decided that,' smiled Glogauer.

John's grim expression softened. He smiled and grasped him by the upper arm in the Roman fashion.

'So – you are our friend. Perhaps more than just our friend...'

Glogauer frowned. 'I do not follow you.' He was relieved that the Baptist, who had plainly spent all this time carefully checking that Glogauer was not in the pay of his enemies, had decided he was a friend.

'I think you know what I mean,' John said.

Glogauer was tired. He had eaten very little and had spent most of the day in the sun, tending the goats. He yawned and could not bring himself to pursue the question.

'I do not...' he began.

John's face clouded for a moment, then he laughed awkwardly. 'Say nothing now. Eat with me tonight. I have wild honey and locusts.'

Glogauer had not yet eaten this food, which was the staple of travellers who did not carry provisions but lived off the food they could find on the journey. Some regarded it as a delicacy.

'Thank you,' he said. 'Tonight.'

John smiled at him, a mysterious smile, then strode on, followed by his men.

Puzzling, Glogauer drove the goats into their caves and closed the wicker gate to keep them in. Then he crossed the clearing to his own cave and lay down on the straw.

Evidently the Baptist saw him as fulfilling some rôle in his own scheme of things.

All the grass, all the trees, all the sunny days with Eva, sweet, virginal, admiring. He had met her in Oxford at a party given by Gerard Friedman, the journalist who specialised in books on the supernatural.

The next day they had walked beside the Isis, looking at the barges moored on the opposite bank, the boys fishing, the spires of the colleges in the distance.

She was concerned.

'You mustn't worry so much, Karl. Nothing's perfect. Can't you take life as it comes?'

She was the first girl who had ever made him feel relaxed. He had laughed. 'I suppose so. Why not?'

She was so warm. Her blonde hair was long and fine, often falling over her face, hiding her large blue eyes that were always so candid, whether she was serious or amused.

For those few weeks he had taken life as it came. They slept together in his little attic room at Friedman's place, not even disturbed by Friedman's salacious interest in their affair, unbothered by the letters she sometimes received from her parents asking her when she was coming home.

She was eighteen, in her first year at Somerville, and it was vacation time.

It was the first time he could ever remember being loved by anyone. She was completely in love with him and he with her. At first her passion and her concern for him had embarrassed him, made him feel suspicious, for he could not believe that anyone could feel such love for him. Gradually he had accepted it, returned it. When apart they wrote not very good love poetry to each other.

'You're so good, Karl,' she would say. 'You'll really do something marvellous in the world.'

He would laugh. 'The only talent I've got is for self-pity...'

'Self-awareness – that's different.'

He would try to argue her out of her idealised picture of him, but this only convinced her of his modesty.

'You're like – like Parsifal...' she told him one night, and he laughed aloud, saw that he had hurt her and kissed her on the forehead.

'Don't be silly, Eva.'

'I mean it, Karl. You're looking for the Holy Grail. And you'll find it.'

He had been impressed by her faith in him, began to wonder if she were right. Perhaps he did have a destiny. She made him feel so heroic. He basked in her worship.

He did some research work for Friedman and earned enough money to buy her a small silver ankh to hang about her neck. She had been delighted by it. She was studying Comparative Religion and was at that time particularly enthusiastic about the Egyptians.

But he was not content for long to enjoy her love for him. He had to test it; make sure of it. He began to get drunk in the evenings, telling her dirty stories, picking fights in pubs – fights, he made it plain, that he was too cowardly to follow through with.

And she began to withdraw from him.

'You're making me nervous,' she explained sorrowfully. 'You make me feel so tense.'

'What's the matter? Can't you love me for myself? This is what I'm like, you know. I'm not Parsifal.'

'You're letting yourself down, Karl.'

'I'm just trying to show you what I'm really like.'

'But you're not really like that. You're sweet – good – kind...'

'I'm a self-pitying failure. Take it or leave it.'

She left it. She went home to her parents two days later. He wrote to her and received no reply. He went to see her and her parents said she was out.

For several months he was filled with a terrible sense of loss, of bewilderment. Why had he deliberately destroyed their relationship? Because he wanted her to accept him as he was, not as she imagined him to be. But suppose she were right? Had he deliberately rejected the chance to be something better? He could not tell.

One of the Baptist's followers came for him an hour later and led him to the house on the other side of the valley.

There were only two rooms in the house: one for eating and one for sleeping.

John greeted him in the barely furnished dining room. He gestured for him to sit on the cotton mat on the other side of the low table on which the food had been placed.

He sat down and crossed his legs. On the other side of the table John smiled and waved his hand at the food. 'Begin.'

The honey-and-locusts was too sweet for his taste, but it was a welcome change from barley or goat meat.

John the Baptist ate with relish. Night had fallen and the room was lit by lamps consisting of wicks floating in bowls of oil. From outside came low murmurs and the moans and cries of those at prayer.

Glogauer dipped another locust into the bowl of honey. 'Why did you wish to see me, John?'

'Because it is time.'

'Time for what? Do you plan to lead the people of Judaea in revolt against the Romans?'

The Baptist seemed disturbed by the direct question. It was the first of its nature that Glogauer had put to him.

'If it be Adonai's will,' he said, not looking up as he leaned towards the bowl of honey.

'The Romans know this?'

'I am not sure, Emmanuel, but Herod the incestuous has doubtless told them I speak against the unrighteous.'

'Yet the Romans do not arrest you.'

'Pilate dare not – not since the petition was sent to the Emperor Tiberius.'

'Petition?'

'Aye, the one that Herod and the Pharisees signed when Pilate the procurator did place votive shields in the palace of Jerusalem and seek to violate the Temple. Tiberius rebuked Pilate and since then, though he still hates the Jews, the procurator is more careful in his treatment of us.'

'Tell me, John, do you know how long Tiberius has ruled in Rome?' He had not had the chance to ask the question again until now.

'Fourteen years.'

It was AD 28 – something less than a year before the date when most scholars agreed that the crucifixion had taken place, and his time machine was smashed.

Now John the Baptist planned armed rebellion against the occupying Romans, but, if the Gospels were to be believed, would soon be decapitated by Herod. Certainly no large-scale rebellion had taken place at this time.

Even those who claimed that the entry of Jesus and his disciples into Jerusalem and the invasion of the Temple were plainly the actions of armed rebels had found no records to suggest that John had led a similar revolt.

Once again it occurred to him that he could warn John. But would the Baptist believe him? Would he choose not to believe him, whatever evidence was presented?

Glogauer had come to like the Baptist very much. The man was plainly a hardened revolutionary who had been planning revolt against the Romans for years and had slowly been building up enough followers to make the attempt successful.

He reminded Glogauer strongly of a type of resistance leader of the Second World War. He had a similar toughness and understanding of the realities of his position. He knew that he would only have one chance to smash the cohorts garrisoned in the country. If the revolt became protracted, Rome would have ample time to send more troops to Jerusalem.

'When do you think Adonai intends to destroy the unrighteous through your agency?' Glogauer asked tactfully.

John glanced at him with some amusement.

'The Passover is a time when the people are restless and resent the strangers most,' he said.

'When is the next Passover?'

'Not for many months.'

Glogauer ate in silence for a while, then he looked up frankly at the Baptist.

'I play some part in this, don't I?' he said.

John looked at the ground. 'You were sent by Adonai to help us accomplish his will.'

'How can I help you?'

'You are a magus.'

'I can work no miracles.'

John wiped honey from his beard. 'I cannot believe that, Emmanuel. The manner of your coming was miraculous. The Essenes did not know if you were a devil or a messenger from Adonai.'

'I am neither.'

'Why do you confuse me, Emmanuel? I know that you are Adonai's messenger. You are the sign that the Essenes sought. The time is almost ready. The kingdom of heaven shall soon be established on earth. Come with us. Tell the people that you speak with Adonai's voice. Work great miracles.'

'Your power is waning, is that it?' Glogauer looked sharply at John. 'You need me to renew your rebels' hopes?'

'You speak like a Roman, with such lack of subtlety!' John got up angrily.

Evidently, like the Essenes he lived with, he preferred less direct methods of expression. There was a practical reason for this, Glogauer realised, in that John and his men feared betrayal all the time. Even the Essenes' records were partially written in cipher, with one innocent-seeming word or phrase meaning something else entirely.

'I am sorry, John. But tell me if I am right.' Glogauer spoke softly.

'Are you not a magus, coming in that chariot from nowhere?' The Baptist waved his hands and shrugged his shoulders. 'My men saw you! They saw the shining thing take shape in air, crack and let you enter out of it. Is that not magical? The clothing you wore – was that earthly raiment? The talismans within the char-iot – did they not speak of powerful magic? The prophet said that a magus would come from Egypt and be called Emmanuel. So it is written in the Book of Micah! Are none of these things true?'

'Most of them. But there are explanations –' He broke off, unable to think of the nearest word to 'rational'. 'I am an ordinary man, like you. I have no power to work miracles! I am just a man!'

John glowered. 'You mean you refuse to help us?'

'I'm grateful to you and the Essenes. You saved my life almost certainly. If I can repay that…'

John nodded his head deliberately. 'You can repay it, Emmanuel.'

'How?'

'Be the great magus I need. Let me present you to all those who become impatient and would turn away from Adonai's will. Let me tell them the manner of your coming to us. Then you can say that all is Adonai's will and that they must prepare to accom-plish it.'

John gave him an intense stare.

'Will you, Emmanuel?'

'John – there is no way in which I can help you without deceiv-ing you, or myself, or the people…'

John looked at him thoughtfully. 'Perhaps you are unaware of your destiny…' he said musingly. 'Why should you not be? Indeed, if you made great claims I would be much more suspicious of you. Emmanuel, will you not take my word that you are the one whom it was prophesied would come?'

Glogauer felt defeated. How could he argue against that? For all he knew, he could be the one. Suppose there were men gifted with some sort of clairvoyant powers… Oh, it was nonsense. Yet what could he do?

'John, you are desperate for a sign. Suppose the true magus arrives…'

'He has arrived. You are he. I have prayed and I know.'

How could he suggest to John that it was his desperate need for help which had probably convinced him? He sighed.

'Emmanuel – will you not help the people of Judaea?'

44

Glogauer pursed his lips. 'Let me think, John. Let me sleep. Come to me in the morning and I will tell you then.'

With some surprise he realised that their rôles had changed. Now instead of wishing to keep the Baptist's good will, the Baptist was anxious to keep his.

When he returned to his cave he felt exhilarated, could not stop himself from smiling broadly. Without engineering it at all, he was now in a position of power. How should he use the power? Did he really have a mission? Could he alter history and be the one responsible for aiding the Jews to throw out the Romans?

Chapter Six

'TO BE JEWISH is to be immortal,' Friedman had told him a few days after Eva had gone back to her parents. 'To be Jewish is to have a destiny – even if that destiny is simply to survive.'

Friedman was tall and bulky with a pale, fat face and cynical eyes. He was almost completely bald. He wore heavy suits of green tweed. He was extremely generous to Karl and appeared to expect little in return – only Karl as an audience occasionally.

'To be Jewish is to be a martyr. Have some more sherry.' He crossed his study and poured another large glass for Karl. 'That's where you went wrong with her, my boy. You couldn't stand the success.'

'I'm not sure that's true, Gerard. I wanted her to take me as I was –'

'You wanted her to take you as you saw yourself, not as she saw you. Who's to say who's right? You do see yourself as a martyr, don't you? What a pity. A lovely girl like that. You might've passed her on to me instead of frightening her off.'

'Oh, don't, Gerard. I loved her!'

'Loved yourself more.'

'Who doesn't?'

'Lots of people have no love for themselves at all. It's to your credit that you do love yourself.'

'You make me sound like Narcissus.'

'You haven't the looks. Don't kid yourself.'

'Anyway, I don't think it's anything at all to do with being Jewish. You and your generation always make a big mystique out of being a Jew. You're over-compensating for what happened under Hitler.'

'Possibly.'

'Anyway, I'm not really a Jew. I wasn't brought up Jewish.'

'With that mother of yours, you weren't brought up Jewish! Maybe you didn't go to the synagogue, son, but you got the lot otherwise…'

'Oh, Gerard. Anyway, you're obscuring the issue – I'm trying to think how to get her back.'

'Forget her. Find yourself a nice Jewish girl. I mean it. She'll understand you. When all's said and done, Karl, these Nordic types are no good for what you want…'

'Christ! I didn't know you were a racialist.'

'I'm just a realist…'

'I've heard that before.'

'All right. If you want trouble…'

'Maybe I do.'

Father…

Pained eyes.

Father…

A mouth moving. No words.

Heavy wooden cross struggling in a swamp while on a hillock a delicate silver cross watched.

Hel… NO!

Mustn't ask…

Just want… NO!

HELP ME!

no

'Formal religion's no good,' Johnny told him in the pub. Johnny was an undergraduate friend of Gerard's. 'It just doesn't suit the times. You've got to find the answer in yourself. Meditation.'

Johnny was thin, with a perpetually worried face. According to Gerard, he was in his third year and doing very badly.

'You get the comforts of religion without the responsibility,' said Friedman from where he sat on a bar-stool just behind Johnny.

Karl laughed.

Johnny rounded on Gerard. 'That's typical, isn't it? You don't know what you're talking about. Responsibility? I'm a pacifist – ready to die for my beliefs. That's more than you'd do!'

'I haven't any beliefs –'

'Exactly!'

Karl laughed again. 'I'll passively resist any man in this pub!'

'Oh, shut up! I've found something neither of you'll ever find.'

'Doesn't seem to have done you much good,' Karl said cruelly, regretted it and put his hand on Johnny's shoulder, but the young man shrugged it off and left the pub.

Karl became very depressed.

'Don't worry about Johnny,' said Gerard. 'He's always being baited.'

'It's not that really. He was right. He's got something he believes in. I can't seem to find anything.'

'It's healthier.'

'I don't know how you can talk about health, with your morbid interest in witch covens and stuff…'

'We've all got our problems,' said Gerard. 'Have another.'

Karl frowned. 'I only attacked Johnny because he embarrassed me, showed me up in a way.'

'We've all got our problems. Have another.'

'All right.'

Trapped. Sinking. Can't be myself. Made into what other people expect. Is that everyone's fate? Were the great individualists the products of their friends who wanted a great individualist as a friend?

Great individuals must be lonely. Everyone needs to think they're invulnerable. In the end they're treated less like human beings than anyone. Treated as symbols of something that can't exist. They must be lonely.

Lonely.

There's always a reason to be lonely.

Lonely…

★

'Mum – I want…'

'Who wants to know what you want? Been away nearly a year. Never wrote. What about what I want? Where were you? I could have died…'

'Try to understand me…'

'Why should I? Have you ever tried to understand me?'

'I've tried, yes…'

'Like hell. What do you want this time?'

'I want…'

'Did I tell you what the doctor told me…?'

Lonely…

I need…

I want…

'You don't get anything in this world that you haven't earned. And you don't always get what you've earned, either.'

Drunk, he leaned against the bar and watched the little red-faced man talk.

'There's a lot of people don't get what they deserve,' said the publican and laughed.

'What I mean is,' said the red-faced man slowly.

'Why don't you shut up?' said Karl.

'Shut up yourself.'

'Oh, shut up both of you,' said the publican.

Love…

Delicate. Tender. Sweet.

Love…

'Your trouble, Karl,' said Gerard as they walked along the High towards the Mitre where Gerard had decided to buy Karl lunch, 'is that you're hung up on romantic love. Look at me, I've got all kinds of kinks… as you're so fond of pointing out in that hectoring voice of yours. I get terribly randy watching black masses and all that. But I don't go around butchering virgins – partly because it's against the law. But you romantic-love perverts – there's no law to stop you. I can't do it unless she's wearing a black veil or something, but you can't do it unless you've sworn undying love and she's sworn undying love back and everything's horribly mixed up. The damage you do! To yourself and the poor girls you use! It's disgusting…'

'You're being more cynical than usual, Gerard.'

'No! Not a bit of it. I speak with absolute sincerity – I've never felt so passionate about anything in my life! Romantic love! There really ought to be some law against it. Disgusting. Disastrous. Look what happened to Romeo and Juliet. There's a warning there for all of us.'

'Oh, Gerard…'

'Why can't you just fuck and enjoy it? Leave it at that. Take it for granted. Don't pervert some poor girl, too.'

'They're usually the ones who want it that way.'

'You have a point, dear boy.'

'Don't you believe in love at all, Gerard?'

'My dear Karl, if I didn't believe in some kind of love, would I be bothering to give you this warning?'

Karl smiled at him. 'You're very kind, Gerard…'

'Oh, good God! Don't, Karl, please! You see what I mean? If you look at me like that once more, I shall not buy you that expensive lunch. I'm serious.'

Karl sighed. The only man who had ever seemed to show him any disinterested affection was the only man who refused to allow him any display of affection. It was ironic, really.

I want…

I need…

I want…

'Monica. There's something lacking in *me*…'

'What sort of a lack?'

'Well, perhaps it's more a sort of a lack of a lack, if you know what I mean.'

'Oh, for Christ's sake!'

★

'You're sensitive,' Eva had told him.

'No, I told you – self-pitying. It passes for sensitivity.'

'Oh, Karl. Why don't you allow yourself some mercy?'

'Mercy? I don't deserve it.'

'What are you looking for, Karl?' Gerard asked over lunch.

'I don't know. Perhaps the Holy Grail. Eva seemed to think I'd find it.'

'Why not? It'd be worth a fortune these days! Shall we have another bottle?'

'You know, I'm not a martyr, Gerard, I'm not a saint, I'm not a hero, I'm not really a bum. I'm just me. Why can't people take me like that?'

'Karl – I like you for being exactly yourself.'

'So you can patronise me. You like me mixed up, you mean.'

'You may be right. Another bottle?'

'All right.'

Gerard had offered to pay his fees so that he could study psychology.

'I'm only doing it because I'm alarmed at what might otherwise happen to you,' he said. 'You might enter the Catholic Church at this rate!'

He had taken the course for a year before drifting out of it. All he had wanted to do was study Jung and they had insisted on his making a variety of studies. He found most of the rest of them very unsympathetic.

God?

God?

God?

No reply.

With Gerard he was serious, intense, intelligent.

With Johnny he was superior, mocking.

With some he was quiet. With others, noisy. In the company of fools, he was happy as a fool. In the company of those he admired, he was pleased if he could sound astute.

'Why am I all things to all men, Gerard? I'm just not sure who I am. Which of those people am I, Gerard? What's wrong with me?'

'Maybe you're just a bit too eager to please, Karl.'

Chapter Seven

H E HAD MET Monica again in the summer of 1962, shortly after he had given up his studies. He was doing all sorts of temporary work and his spirits were very low.

At that time Monica had seemed a great help, a great guide through the mental darkness engulfing him.

They both lived close to Holland Park and it was there that they had met one Sunday, by the goldfish pond in the ornamental garden.

They went to Holland Park for walks almost every Sunday of that summer. He was by that time completely obsessed with Jung's strange brand of Christian mysticism.

She, who despised Jung, had soon begun to denigrate all his ideas.

Although she never really convinced him, she had soon succeeded in confusing him.

It would be another six months before they went to bed together.

He woke up to see John standing over him. The Baptist had an expression of anxious concern on his bearded features.

'Well, Emmanuel?'

Karl scratched at his own beard. He nodded his head. 'Very well, John. I will help you for your sake, because you befriended me and saved my life. But in return, will you send men to bring my chariot here as soon as possible? I wish to see if it can be mended.'

'I will.'

'You must not have too much faith in my powers, John...'

'I have absolute faith in them...'

'I hope you will not be disappointed.'

'I will not be.' John put his hand on Glogauer's arm. 'You shall baptise me on the morrow, to show all the people that Adonai is with us.'

He was still worried by the Baptist's faith in his powers, but there was nothing more he could say. If others shared the Baptist's faith, then possibly he could do something.

Glogauer felt the exhilaration of the night before, and the broad smile came uncontrollably to his lips again.

The Baptist began to laugh, uncertainly at first, but then more spontaneously.

Glogauer, too, began to laugh, unable to stop himself, every so often pausing to gasp for breath.

It was completely incongruous that he should be the one who, with John the Baptist, would prepare the way for Christ.

Christ was not born yet, however.

Perhaps Glogauer was beginning to understand this, one year before the crucifixion.

And the Word was made flesh and dwelt among us (and we beheld his glory, the glory as of the only begotten of the Father) full of grace and truth. John bare witness of him, and cried, saying, This was he of whom I spake, He that cometh after me is preferred before me; for he was before me.

(John 1: 14–15)

It was uncomfortably hot.

They sat in the shade of the cafeteria, watching a distant cricket match.

Nearer to them, two girls and a boy sat on the grass, drinking orange squash from plastic cups. One of the girls had a guitar across her lap and she set the cup down and began to play, singing a folk song in a high, gentle voice.

Karl tried to listen to the words. At the college, he had developed a liking for traditional folk music.

'Christianity is dead.' Monica sipped her tea. 'Religion is dying. God was killed in 1945.'

'There may yet be a resurrection,' he said.

'Let's hope not. Religion was the creation of fear. Knowledge destroys fear. Without fear, religion can't survive.'

'You think there's no fear about these days?'

'Not the same kind, Karl.'

'Haven't you ever considered the *idea* of Christ?' he asked her, changing his tack. 'What that means to Christians?'

'The idea of the tractor means as much to a Marxist,' she replied.

'But what came first? The idea or the actuality of Christ?'

She shrugged. 'The actuality, if it matters. Jesus was a Jewish troublemaker organising a revolt against the Romans. He was crucified for his pains. That's all we know and all we need to know.'

'A great religion couldn't have begun so simply.'

'When people need one, they'll make a great religion out of the most unlikely beginnings.'

'That's my point, Monica.' He gesticulated intensely and she drew away slightly. 'The *idea* preceded the *actuality* of Christ.'

'Oh, Karl, don't go on. The actuality of *Jesus* preceded the *idea* of Christ.'

A couple walked past, glancing curiously at them as they argued. Monica noticed them and fell silent.

'Why are you so keen to knock religion, sneer at Jung?' he said.

She got up and he rose as well, but she shook her head.

'I'm going home, Karl. You stay here. I'll see you in a few days.'

He watched her walk down the wide path towards the park gates. Perhaps he enjoyed her company, he thought, because she was prepared to argue as intensely as he did – or almost, anyway.

Vampires.

We're quite a pair.

The next day, when he got home from work, he found a letter.

She must have written it after she had left him, and posted it the same day. He opened it and began to read.

Dear Karl,

Conversation doesn't seem to have much effect on you, you know. It's as if you listen to the tone of the voice, the rhythm of the words, without ever hearing what is trying to be communicated.

You're a bit like a sensitive animal, I suppose, who can't understand what's being said to it, but can tell if the person talking to it is pleased or angry and so on. That's why I'm writing to you – to try to get my idea across. You respond too emotionally when we're together.

He smiled at that. One of the reasons he enjoyed her company so much was because at most times her responses could be counted upon to be passionate.

You make the mistake of considering Christianity as something that developed over the course of a few years, from the death of Jesus to the time the Gospels were written. But Christianity wasn't new. Only the name was new. Christianity was merely a stage in the meeting, cross-fertilisation, metamorphosis of Western logic and Eastern mysticism. Look how the religion itself changed over the centuries, reinterpreting itself to meet changing times. Christianity is just a new name for a conglomeration of old myths and philosophies. All the Gospels do is retell the sun myth and garble some of the ideas from the Greeks and Romans.

Even in the second century, Jewish scholars were showing it up for the mish-mash it was!

They pointed out the strong similarities between the various sun myths and the Christ myth. The miracles didn't happen – they were invented later, borrowed from here and there.

Remember those old Victorian dons who used to argue that Plato was really a Christian because he anticipated Christian thought?

Christian thought!

Christianity was a vehicle for ideas in circulation centuries before Christ. Was Marcus Aurelius a Christian? He was writing in the direct tradition of Western philosophy. That's why Christianity caught on in Europe and not in the East!

You should have been a theologian with your bias – not tried to be a psychologist. The same goes for your friend Jung.

Try to clear your head of all this morbid nonsense and you'll make a much better job of your life.

Yours,
Monica.

He screwed the letter up and threw it away. Later that evening he was tempted to look at it again, but he resisted the temptation.

The time machine seemed unfamiliar. Perhaps because he had become so used to the primitive life of the Essenes, the cracked globe looked as strange to him as it must have done to them.

He touched the stud that would normally have operated the airlock from the outside, but nothing happened.

He crawled in through the crack. All the fluid had gone, as he already knew, and without that to cushion him, any journey through time would probably kill him anyway.

John the Baptist peered in, as if afraid that Glogauer was going to try to make his escape in his chariot.

Glogauer smiled at him. 'Don't worry, John.'

Everything was dead. The motors would not respond and even if he stripped off their casings, he wasn't engineer enough to fix them. None of the instruments was working. The time machine was dead.

Unless Headington built another machine and sent it after him, he was stranded in this period for good.

The understanding came to him as a shock.

He would probably never see the twentieth century again, could not report what he witnessed here.

Tears came to his eyes and he staggered from the machine, pushing John aside.

'What is it, Emmanuel?'

'What am I doing here? What am I doing here?' he cried in English, and the words came thickly. These, too, seemed unfamiliar. What was happening to him?

He began to wonder if this whole thing were not an illusion, some kind of protracted dream. The idea of a time machine now seemed completely ludicrous to him. The thing was an impossibility.

'Oh, God,' he groaned, 'what's going on?'

Again a sense of being completely abandoned came to him.

Chapter Eight

WHERE AM I?
　　　Who am I?
What am I?
Where am I?

'Time and identity,' Headington used to say enthusiastically, 'the two great mysteries. Angles, curves, soft and hard perspectives. What do we see? What are we that we see in a particular way? What could we be or have been? All the twists and turns of time. I loathe those ideas that insist on treating time as a dimension of space, describing it in spacial metaphors. No wonder they get nowhere. Time is nothing to do with space – it is to do with the psyche. Ah! Nobody understands. Not even you!'

The other members of the group had thought of him as a bit of a crank.

'I am the only one,' he had said quietly and earnestly, 'who really understands the nature of time…'

'And on that note…' Mrs Rita Blen said firmly, 'I think it's about time for a cup of tea, don't you?'

The other members agreed enthusiastically.

Mrs Rita Blen had been a little unsubtle. Hurt, Headington had got up and left.

'Oh, well,' she said. 'Oh, well…'

But the others were annoyed with her. Headington was, after all, well known and gave the group a certain prestige.

'I hope he comes back,' Glogauer had murmured.

He had suffered migraine since adolescence. He would become dizzy, vomiting, completely immersed in pain.

Often during the attacks he would begin to assume an identity – a character in a book he was reading, some politician currently in the news, someone in history if he had recently read a biography.

The one thing that marked them all would be their anxieties. Heyst in *Victory* had been obsessed with the three men coming to the island, worrying how to stop them, how to kill them if possible (as Heyst, he had become a somewhat less subtle character than Conrad's). After reading a history of the Russian revolution, he became convinced that his name was Zinoniev, Minister in charge of Transport and Telegraphs, with the responsibility of sorting out the chaos in 1918, knowing, too, that he had to be careful, otherwise he would be purged in a few years' time.

He would lie in a darkened room, his head full of nauseating pain, unable to sleep properly because he could find no solution for the completely hypothetical problems that obsessed him. He would lose track completely of his own identity and circumstances unless someone came to remind him of who and where he was.

Monica had been amused when he told her.

'One day,' she said, 'you'll wake up and ask who you are – and I won't tell you!'

'A fine psychiatric worker you are!' he'd laughed.

Neither of them worried about these mild hallucinations. In his day-to-day life he was not bothered by any abnormally schizoid tendencies, save that his rôle would sometimes change a little to suit the company he kept; he would find himself unconsciously imitating nuances of speech in other people, but he understood that everyone did that to some extent. It was part of life.

Sometimes he wondered about it, wondered at the accretions of other people's personalities upon his own.

Drunk in some pub, he'd suddenly got up from the table and waved his arms, jumping up and down and grinning at Monica. 'Look at me,' he'd said. 'Look – the original coral island...'

She had frowned at him petulantly. 'What are you on about now? You'll get us thrown out.'

'It's only me from over the sea, I'm Barnacle Bill the Sailor,' he sang.

'You can't hold your liquor, Karl, that's your problem…'

'I hold too much – that's my problem.'

''Ere, what d'you think you're playing at?' said a man at the bar whose elbow he had jogged.

'I wish I knew, friend. I wish I knew.'

'Come on, Karl.' She was up, tugging at his arm.

'Every man's life diminishes me,' he said as she dragged him through the doorway.

Pubs and bedrooms; bedrooms and pubs. He seemed to spend most of his life in semi-darkness. Even the bookshop would be dingy.

There had been days out, of course – sunny days and bright winter days – but all his memories of Monica were set against dark backgrounds of one kind or another. Tramping through muddy snow in the park beneath that particularly English sky, that heavy, leaden sky.

Whatever the hour, they had seemed to exist together in the twilight, after those first summer meetings before they slept together.

He had once said: 'I have a twilit mind…'

'If you mean a murky mind, I'm with you there,' she had replied.

He ignored the remark. 'It's my mother, I think. She never really had a firm hold on reality…'

'There's nothing much wrong with you if you'd face up to things – a trifle too much narcissism is all you've got.'

'Someone used to say I had too much self-hatred.'

'Just too much self.'

He would hold his circumcised penis in his hand and look at it with sentimental affection.

'You're the only friend I've got. The only friend I've got.'

Often it would take on a character of its own in his thoughts. A boon friend, the giver of pleasure. A bit of a lad though, always leading him into trouble.

*

Soft silver crosses spreading themselves against the surface of the shining sea.

Plonk!

Wooden crosses fell from the sky.

Plonk!

Disrupting the surface, shaking the silver crucifixes to pieces.

'Why do I destroy everything I love?'

'Oh, God! Don't give me that maudlin teenage stuff, Karl, please!'

Plonk.

Across all the deserts of Arabia I made my way, a slave of the sun, searching for my God.

'Time and identity – the two great mysteries…'

Where am I?

Who am I?

What am I?

Where am I?

Chapter Nine

FIVE YEARS IN the past.

Nearly two thousand in the future.

Lying in the hot, sweaty bed with Monica.

Once again another attempt to make normal love had changed gradually into the performance of minor aberrations which seemed to satisfy her better than anything else.

Their real courtship and fulfilment was yet to come. As usual, it would be verbal. As usual, it would find its climax in argumentative anger.

'I suppose you're going to tell me you're not satisfied again.' She accepted the lighted cigarette he handed to her in the darkness.

'I'm all right,' he said.

There was silence for a while as they smoked.

Eventually, and in spite of knowing what the result would be if he did so, he found himself talking.

'It's ironic, isn't it?' he began.

He waited for her reply. She would delay for a little while yet.

'What is?' she said at last.

'All this. You spend all day trying to help neurotics with their sex problems. You spend your nights doing what they do.'

'Not to the same extent. You know it's all a matter of degree.'

'So you say.'

He turned his head and looked at her face in the starlight from the window.

She was a gaunt-featured redhead, with the calm, professional seducer's voice of the psychiatric social worker. It was a voice that was soft, reasonable, insincere. Only occasionally, when she became particularly agitated, did her voice begin to indicate her real character.

Her features, he thought, never seemed to be in repose, even when she slept. Her eyes were forever wary, her movements rarely spontaneous. Every inch of her was protected, which was probably why she got so little pleasure from ordinary love-making.

He sighed.

'You just can't let yourself go, can you?'

'Oh, shut up, Karl. Have a look at yourself if you're looking for a neurotic mess.'

They used the terminology of psychiatry freely. Both felt happier if they could name something.

He rolled away from her, groping for the ashtray on the bedside table, catching a glimpse of himself in the dressing-table mirror.

He was a sallow, intense, moody Jewish cleric, with a head full of images and unresolved obsessions, a body full of conflicting emotions. He always lost these arguments with Monica. Verbally, at very least, she was the dominant one.

This kind of exchange often seemed to him more perverse than their love-making, where usually at least his rôle was masculine. At this time he had decided that he was essentially passive, masochistic, indecisive. Even his anger, which came frequently, was these days impotent.

Monica was ten years older than him, ten years more bitter. As an individual, he believed, she had more dynamism than he had. Yet she had a great many failures in her work. She plugged on, however, becoming increasingly cynical on the surface but still, perhaps, hoping for a few spectacular successes with patients.

They tried to do too much, that was the trouble, he thought. The priests in the confessional supplied a panacea; the psychiatrists tried to cure, and most of the time they failed. But at least they tried, he thought, and then wondered if that was, after all, a virtue.

'I did look at myself,' he said.

Was she sleeping?

He turned.

Her wary eyes were still open, looking out of the window.

'I did look at myself,' he repeated. 'The way Jung did. "How can I help those persons if I am myself a fugitive and perhaps also suffer from the *morbus sacer* of a neurosis?" That's what Jung asked himself...'

'That old sensationalist. That old rationaliser of his own mysticism. No wonder you never became a psychiatrist.'

'I wouldn't have been any good. It was nothing to do with Jung...'

'Don't take it out on me...'

'I wanted to help people. I couldn't find a way through. You've told me yourself that you feel the same – you think it's useless.'

'After a hard week's work, I might say that. Give me another fag.'

He opened the packet on the bedside table and put two cigarettes in his mouth, lighting them and handing her one.

Almost unconsciously, he noticed that the tension was increasing.

The argument was, as ever, pointless. But it was not the argument that was the important thing: it was simply the expression of the essential relationship. He wondered if that was in any way important, either.

'You're not telling the truth.' He knew that there would be no stopping now that the ritual was in full swing.

'I'm telling the practical truth. I've no compulsion to give up my work. To drop out. I've no wish to be a failure...'

'Failure? You're more melodramatic than I am!'

'You're too earnest, Karl. You want to get out of yourself a bit.'

He sneered. 'If I were you, I'd give up my work, Monica. You're no more suited for it than I was.'

She shrugged, tugging at the sheets. 'You're a petty bastard.'

'I'm not jealous of you, if that's what you think. You'll never understand what I'm looking for.'

Her laugh was brittle. 'Modern man in search of a soul, eh? Modern man in search of a crutch, I'd say. And you can take that any way you like.'

'We're destroying the myths that make the world go round.'

'Now you say, "And what are we putting in their place?" You're stale and stupid, Karl. You've never looked rationally at anything – including yourself.'

'What of it? You say the myth is unimportant.'

'The reality that creates it is important.'

'Jung knew that the myth can also create the reality.'

'Which shows what a muddled old fool he was.'

He stretched his legs. In doing so, he touched hers and he recoiled. He scratched his head. She still lay there smoking, but she was smiling now.

'Come on,' she said. 'Let's have some stuff about Christ.'

He said nothing.

She handed him the stub of her cigarette and he put it in the ashtray. He looked at his watch.

It was two o'clock in the morning.

'Why do we do it?' he said.

'Because we must.'

She put her hand to the back of his head and pulled it towards her breasts. 'What else can we do?'

He began to cry.

Generous in victory, she stroked his head and murmured to him.

Ten minutes later he made love to her savagely.

Then minutes after that he was crying again.

Betrayal.

He betrayed himself and was thus betrayed.

'I want to help people.'

'You'd better get someone to help you first.'

'Oh, Monica. Monica.'

We Protestants must sooner or later face this question: Are we to understand the 'imitation of Christ' in the sense that we should copy his life and, if I may use the expression, ape his stigmata; or in the deeper sense that we are to live our own proper lives as truly as he lived his in all its implications? It is no easy matter to live a life that

*is modelled on Christ's, but it is unspeakably harder to live one's own
life as truly as Christ lived his. Anyone who did this would ... be
misjudged, derided, tortured and crucified ... A neurosis is a disasso-
ciation of personality.*

(Jung, *Modern Man in Search of a Soul*)

Lonely...
 I am lonely...

'So he's dead, is he? Never sent me a penny while he was alive.
Never came to see you. Now he leaves you a business.'
 'Mum – it's a bookshop. It probably doesn't do very well.'
 'A bookshop! I suppose that's typical of him. A bookshop!'
 'I'll sell it, if you like, Mum – give you the money.'
 'Thanks very much,' she said with irony. 'No, you keep it.
Maybe you'll stop borrowing from me now.'
 'It's funny they didn't write earlier,' he said.
 'They might have invited us to the funeral.'
 'Would you have gone?'
 'He was my husband, wasn't he? Your father.'
 'I suppose it took them a while to find out where we lived.'
 'How many Glogauers are there in London?'
 'True. Come to think of it – it's odd you never heard of him.'
 'Why should I? He wasn't in the phone book. What was the
shop called?'
 'The Mandala Bookshop. It's in Great Russell Street.'
 'Mandala. What sort of a name is that?'
 'It sells books about mysticism and stuff.'
 'Well, you certainly take after him, don't you? I always said you
took after him.'

He picked his way among his father's books. The front part of the
shop was relatively tidy; the books arranged on the shelves that
crowded the small space. The back of the shop, however, was
filled with rocking piles of books that reached to the ceiling, surrounding the untidy desk.

In the cellar there were even more books, stacked one upon the other, with narrow passages winding like a maze between them.

He despaired of tidying the place.

In the end he just left the books as they were, made a few alterations in the main part of the shop, moved a few pieces of his own furniture into the upper part, and then felt settled. What was the point of changing anything?

He came across some privately printed poems under the name of John Fry. The strange girl who worked in the shop told him that they were his father's. He read a few. They were not very good, rather high-flown in their symbolism and imagery, but they revealed a personality so much like his own that he could not bear to read them for long.

'He was a funny old man,' said the fat customer with the drink-flushed face who came in to buy books about black-magic rites. 'A bit barmy in his way, I think. An evil old man, he struck me as. Always shouting at people. The arguments you used to hear from the back of the shop! Did you know him?'

'Not very well,' said Glogauer. 'Fuck off, will you!'

It was the first brave thing he ever remembered doing. He grinned as the man sputtered out of the shop.

His first few months as owner of the shop gave him a sense of stature. But as the bills came in and difficult customers had to be dealt with, the feeling gradually wore off.

He awoke in the cave and said aloud, 'I've no business being here. My existence here is an impossibility. There is no such thing as time travel.'

He did not succeed in convincing himself. His sleep had been disturbed, full of dreams and memories. He could not even be sure if the memories were exact. Had he really ever existed elsewhere, in another time?

He got up and wrapped his linen loincloth about his waist, going to the entrance of the cave.

The morning sky was grey and the sun had not yet risen. The earth was cold under his bare feet as he walked towards the river.

He reached the river and bent to wash his face, seeing his reflection in the dark water. His hair was long, black and matted, his beard covering the whole of his lower face, his eyes slightly mad. There was nothing at all to distinguish him from any one of the Essenes, save his thoughts. And the thoughts of many of the Essenes were strange enough. Were they any wilder than his belief that he was a visitor from a future century?

He shuddered as he splashed cold water on his face.

There was the time machine. He had seen that only yesterday. That was proof.

This sort of speculation was nonsense, anyway, he thought, straightening. It got you nowhere. It was self-indulgent.

On the other hand, what of John's belief that he was a great magus? Was it right to go along with him, let him believe he had the powers of a seer? And was it right that John should use him to restore the flagging faith of those who awaited revolution?

It didn't matter. He was here, this was happening to him, there was nothing he could do about it. He had to stay alive, if possible, so that in a year he could witness the crucifixion, if it did, indeed, take place.

Why did the crucifixion in particular obsess him? Why should that be proof of Christ's divinity? It would not be, of course, but it would enable him to get the feel of what had really happened, what the people had really felt.

Was Christ like John the Baptist? Or a subtler politician, working chiefly in the cities, making friends in the Establishment? And working secretly – for John had not heard of him and John of all people should have known, for he was supposed to be Jesus' cousin.

Perhaps, Glogauer thought, he was mixing with the wrong company.

He smiled and turned back towards the village. He felt tense suddenly. Something dramatic was going to happen today, something that was to decide his future for him. For some reason, however, he rebelled against the idea of baptising the Baptist. It was wrong. He had no right to pose as a great prophet.

He rubbed at his head. There was a slight ache there. He hoped it would go before he saw John.

> *Our birth is but a sleep and a forgetting…*
> (Wordsworth)

The cave was warm, and thick with his memories and thoughts. He entered it with some relief.

Later, he would leave it for the last time.

Then there would be no escape.

'All of us choose our archetypal rôles quite early in life,' he told the group. 'And do not be deceived by the grand term "archetype" – for it applies as much to the bank clerk living in Shepperton as it does to the great figures of history – "archetypal" does not mean "heroic" really. That bank clerk's inner life is as rich as yours or mine, the rôle he sees himself as fulfilling is quite as important to him as anyone else's. Though his suburban suit may deceive you – and deceive those he lives and works with – he –'

'Nonsense, nonsense,' said Sandra Peterson, waving her heavy arms. 'They're not bloody archetypes – they're stereotypes…'

'There is no such thing,' Glogauer insisted. 'It's inhuman to judge people in that way…'

'I don't know what you call it, but I know that these people are the grey ones – the forces of mediocrity who try to drag the others down!'

Glogauer was shocked, almost in tears. 'Really, Sandra, I'm trying to explain –'

'I'm sure you're completely misinterpreting Jung,' she said firmly. 'I've studied everything he wrote!'

'I think Sandra's got a point,' said Mrs Rita Blen. 'After all – this sort of thing is what we're here to thrash out, isn't it?'

It might work.

He had timed it right.

The gas fire was on when Monica got to the flat over the bookshop. The smell of gas filled the room. He lay near the fire.

She opened a window, then crossed to where he lay.

'God, Karl, what you'll do to get attention.'

He began to laugh.

'Jesus. Am I so transparent?'

'I'm off,' she said.

She didn't call for nearly a fortnight. He knew she would. After all, she was getting on, and she wasn't that attractive. She only had him.

'I love you, Monica,' he said as he crawled into bed beside her.

She had her pride. She made no response.

John stood outside the cave now. He was calling to him.

'It is time, magus.'

Reluctantly, he left the cave. He looked appealingly at the Baptist.

'John – are you sure?'

The Baptist turned and began to march towards the river.

'Come. They are waiting.'

'My life's a mess, Monica.'

'Isn't everyone's, Karl?'

Part Two

Chapter Ten

And thine the Human Face, and thine
The Human Hands and Feet and Breath,
Entering thro' the Gates of Birth
And passing thro' the Gates of Death.

(William Blake, *Jerusalem*: 'To the Jews')

JOHN WAS UP to his waist in the sluggish waters of the river. All the Essenes had come to witness his baptism. They stood on the banks, making no sound.

Balanced in the sandy soil between the top of the bank and the water, Glogauer looked down at him and spoke in his odd, heavily accented Aramaic.

'John, I cannot. It is not for me to do it.'

The Baptist frowned. 'You must.'

Glogauer began to gasp, his eyes filling with tears as he gave John a look of agonised appeal.

But the Baptist showed him no mercy.

'You must. It is your duty.'

Glogauer felt light-headed as he lowered himself into the river beside the Baptist. He shivered.

He stood in the water trembling, unable to move.

His foot slipped on the rocks on the river-bottom and John reached out and gripped his arm, steadying him.

In the clear, harsh sky, the sun was at zenith, beating down on his unprotected head.

'Emmanuel!' John cried suddenly. 'The spirit of Adonai is within you!'

Glogauer was startled. 'What…?' he said in English. He blinked rapidly.

'The spirit of Adonai is within you, Emmanuel!'

Glogauer still found it hard to speak. He shook his head slightly. The headache had not worn off and now the pain was growing. He could hardly see. He knew he was having his first migraine attack since he had come here.

He wanted to vomit.

John's voice sounded distorted, distant.

He swayed in the water.

As he began to fall towards the Baptist, the whole scene around him became indistinct.

He felt John catch him and heard himself say desperately: 'John – you must baptise *me*!' And then there was water in his mouth and throat and he was coughing.

He had not felt this kind of panic since the night he had first gone to bed with Monica and thought he was impotent.

John's voice was crying something.

Whatever the words were, they drew a response from the people on the banks.

The roaring in his ears increased, its quality changing. He thrashed in the water, then felt himself lifted to his feet.

Still the pain and panic filled him. He began to vomit into the water, stumbling as John's hands gripped his arms painfully and guided him up the bank.

He had let John down.

'I'm sorry,' he said. 'I'm sorry. I'm sorry. I'm sorry…'

He had lost John his chance of victory. 'I'm sorry. I'm sorry.'

Again, he had not had the strength to do the right thing. 'I'm sorry.'

A peculiar rhythmic humming came from the mouths of the Essenes as they swayed; it rose as they swayed to one side, fell as they swayed to the other.

As John released him, Glogauer covered his ears. He was still retching, but it was dry now, and worse than ever.

He staggered away, barely keeping his balance, running, with his ears still covered; running over the rocky scrubland; running as the sun throbbed in the sky and its heat pounded at his head; running away.

But John forbade him, saying, I have need to be baptised of thee, and comest thou to me? And Jesus answering said unto him, Suffer it to be so now: for thus it becometh us to fulfil all righteousness. Then he suffered him. And Jesus, when he was baptised, went up straightway out of the water: and, lo, the heavens were opened unto him, and he saw the Spirit of God descending like a dove, and lighting upon him: And lo a voice from heaven, saying, This is my beloved Son, in whom I am well pleased.

(Matthew 3: 14–17)

He had been fifteen, doing quite well at the grammar school.

He had read in the newspapers about the Teddy Boy gangs that roamed South London, but the occasional youth he had seen in pseudo-Edwardian clothes had seemed harmless and stupid enough.

He had gone to the pictures in Brixton Hill and decided to walk home to Streatham because he had spent most of the bus money on ice-cream.

They came out of the cinema at the same time. He hardly noticed them as they followed him down the hill.

Then, quite suddenly, they had surrounded him.

They were pale, mean-faced boys, most of them a year or two older than he. He realised that he knew two of them vaguely. They were at the big council school in the same street as the grammar school. They used the same football ground.

'Hello,' he said weakly.

'Hello, son,' said the oldest Teddy Boy. He was chewing gum, standing with one knee bent, grinning at him. 'Where you going, then?'

'Home.'

'Heouwm,' said the biggest one, imitating his accent.

'What are you going to do when you get there?'

'Go to bed.'

Karl tried to get through the ring, but they wouldn't let him.

They pressed him back into a shop doorway. Behind them, cars droned by on the main road. The street was brightly lit, with streetlamps and neon from the shops.

Several people passed, but none of them stopped. Karl began to feel panic.

'Got no homework to do, son?' said the boy next to the leader. He was red-headed and freckled and his eyes were a hard grey.

'Want to fight one of us?' another boy asked. It was one of the boys Karl had recognised.

'No. I don't fight. Let me go.'

'You scared, son?' said the leader, grinning. Ostentatiously, he pulled a streamer of gum from his mouth and then replaced it. He began chewing again, the grin still on his face.

'No. Why should I want to fight you? I don't think anyone should fight.'

'You haven't got much choice, have you, son?'

'Look, I'm late. I've got to get back.'

'You got time for a few rounds…'

'I told you. I don't want to fight you.'

'You reckon you're better than us, is that it, son?'

'No.' He was beginning to tremble. Tears were coming into his eyes. 'Of course not.'

''Course not, son.'

He moved forward again, but they pushed him back into the doorway.

'You're the bloke with the kraut name, ain't you?' said the other boy he knew. 'Glow-worm or somethink.'

'Glogauer. Let me go.'

'Won't your mummy like it if you're back late?'

'More a yid name than a kraut name.'

'You a yid, son?'

'He looks like a yid.'

'You a yid, son?'

'You a Jewish boy, son?'

'You a yid, son?'

'Shut up!' Karl screamed. 'Why are you picking on me?'

He pushed into them. One of them punched him in the stomach. He grunted with pain. Another pushed him and he staggered.

People were still hurrying by on the pavement. Some of them glanced at the group as they went past.

One man stopped, but his wife pulled him on. 'Just some kids larking about,' she said.

'Get his trousers down,' one of the boys suggested with a laugh. 'That'll prove it.'

Karl pushed through them and this time they didn't resist.

He began to run down the hill.

'Give him a start,' he heard one of the boys say.

He ran on.

They began to follow him, laughing and jeering.

They did not catch up with him by the time he turned into the avenue where he lived. Perhaps they hadn't intended to catch him. He blushed.

He reached the house and ran along the dark passage beside it. He opened the back door. His mother was in the kitchen.

'What's the matter with you?' she said.

She was a tall, thin woman, nervous and hysterical. Her dark hair was untidy.

He went past her into the breakfast-room.

'What's the matter, Karl?' she called. Her voice was high-pitched.

'Nothing,' he said.

He didn't want a scene.

Chapter Eleven

I T WAS COLD when he woke up. The false dawn was grey and he could see nothing but barren country in all directions. He could remember very little about the previous day, except that he had let John down somehow and had run a long way.

He was dazed. His skull felt empty. The back of his neck still ached.

Dew had gathered on his loincloth. He unwrapped it and wet his lips, rubbing the material over his face.

As always after a migraine attack he felt weak and completely drained mentally and physically.

Looking down at his naked body, he noticed how skinny he had become.

'I'm like a Belsen victim,' he thought.

He wondered why he had panicked so much when John had asked him to baptise him. Was it simply honesty – something in him which resisted deceiving the Essenes at the very last minute? It was hard to know.

He wrapped the torn loincloth about his hips and tied it tightly just above his left thigh. He supposed he had better try to get back to the camp and find John and apologise, ask if he could make amends.

Then, perhaps, he would move on.

The time machine was still in the Essene village. If a good blacksmith could be found, or some other metal-worker, perhaps there was a chance that it could be repaired. It was a faint hope. Even if it could be patched together, the journey back would be dangerous.

He wondered if he ought to go back right away, or try to shift to a time nearer to the actual crucifixion. It was important that he experience the mood of Jerusalem during the Feast of the Passover, when Jesus was supposed to have entered the city.

Monica had thought Jesus had stormed the city with an armed band. She had said that all the evidence pointed to that.

All the evidence of one sort did point to it, he supposed, but he could not accept the evidence. There was more to it, he was sure.

If only he could meet Jesus.

John had apparently never heard of him, though he had mentioned that there was a prophecy that the Messiah would be a Nazarene.

But there were many prophecies and many of them conflicted.

He began to walk in what he assumed to be the general direction of the Essene village. He could not have come very far.

By noon it had become much hotter and the ground more barren. His eyes were screwed up against the glare and the air shimmered. The feeling of exhaustion with which he had awakened had increased; his skin burned, his mouth was dry and his legs would hardly hold him. He was hungry and he was thirsty and there was nothing to eat or drink. There was no sign of the range of hills where the Essenes had their village.

He was lost and he hardly cared. In his mind he had almost become one with the desert landscape. If he perished here, the transition between life and death would barely be felt. He would lie down and his body would merge with the brown ground.

Mechanically, he moved on through the desert.

Later he saw a hill about two miles away to the south. The sight brought a small return of consciousness. He decided to head for it. From there he would probably be able to get his bearings, perhaps even see a township where they would give him food and water.

He rubbed at his forehead and eyes, but the touch of his own hand was painful to him. He began to plod towards the hill.

The sandy soil turned to floating dust around him as his feet disturbed it. The few primitive shrubs clinging to the ground tore at his ankles and calves, and the jutting rocks tripped him.

He was bleeding and bruised by the time he reached the slopes of the hill.

He rested for a while, staring vaguely around him at the almost featureless landscape, then he began to clamber up the hillside.

The journey to the summit (which was much further away than he had originally judged) was difficult.

He would slide on the loose stones of the hillside, falling on his face, bracing his torn hands and feet to stop himself from sliding down to the bottom, clinging to the tufts of grass and lichen that grew here and there, embracing larger projections of rock when he could, resting frequently, his mind and body both numb with pain and weariness.

He forgot why he climbed, but he became, like some barely sentient life form, determined to reach the summit. Like a beetle, he dragged himself up the mountain.

He sweated beneath the sun. The dust stuck to the moisture on his near-naked body, caking him from head to foot. His loincloth was in shreds.

The barren world reeled around him, sky somehow merging with land, yellow rock with white clouds. Nothing seemed still.

He fell and his body slid down the mountain. His thigh was gashed, his head badly bruised.

As soon as he stopped sliding, he began to climb again, crawling slowly up the burning rock.

Time had become meaningless, identity meaningless. Now, for the first time, he was in a position to appreciate Headington's theories, but consciousness had disappeared also. He was a thing that moved up the mountain.

He reached the summit and stopped crawling.

For a little while he lay there blinking, and then his eyes closed.

He heard Monica's voice and raised his head. For a moment he thought he glimpsed her from the corner of his eye.

Don't be melodramatic, Karl...

She had said that many times. His own voice replied now.

I'm born out of my time, Monica. This age of reason has no place for me. It will kill me in the end.

82

Her voice replied.

Guilt and fear and cowardice and your own masochism. You could have been a brilliant psychiatrist, but you've given in to all your own neuroses so completely...

'Shut up!'

He rolled over on his back. The sun blazed down on his tattered body.

'Shut up!'

The whole Christian syndrome, Karl. You'll become a Catholic convert next, I shouldn't doubt. Where's your strength of mind?

'Shut up! Go away, Monica!'

Fear shapes your thoughts. You're not searching for a soul or even a meaning for life. You're searching for comfort.

'Leave me alone, Monica!'

His filthy hands covered his ears. His hair and beard were matted with dust. Blood had congealed on the wounds that were now on every part of his body. Above, the sun seemed to pound in unison with his heartbeats.

You're going downhill, Karl, don't you realise that? Downhill. Pull yourself together. You're not entirely incapable of rational thought...

'Oh, Monica! Shut up!'

His voice was harsh and cracked.

A few ravens circled the sky above him now. He heard them calling back at him in a voice not unlike his own.

God died in 1945...

'It isn't 1945 – it's AD 28. God is alive!'

How you can bother to wonder about an obvious syncretistic religion like Christianity – rabbinic Judaism, Stoic ethics, Greek mystery cults. Oriental ritual...

'It doesn't matter!'

Not to you in your present state of mind.

'I need God!'

That's what it boils down to, doesn't it? An inadequate human being always ends up like you. Okay, Karl, carve your own crutches. Just think what you could have been if you'd come to terms with yourself...

Glogauer pulled his ruined body to its feet and stood on the summit of the hill and screamed.

The ravens were startled. They wheeled in the sky and flew away.

The sky was darkening now.

Then was Jesus led up of the Spirit into the wilderness to be tempted of the devil. And when he had fasted forty days and forty nights, he was afterward an hungred.

(Matthew 4: 1–2)

Chapter Twelve

T HE MADMAN CAME stumbling into town.

His head was turned upward to face the sun; his eyes rolled; his arms were limp at his sides and his lips moved wordlessly.

His feet stirred the dust and made it dance and dogs barked around him as he walked. Children laughed at him, then they threw pebbles at him, then they crept away.

The madman began to speak.

To the townspeople, the words they heard were in no familiar language; yet they were uttered with such intensity and conviction that God himself might be using this emaciated, naked creature as his spokesman.

They wondered where the madman had come from.

Once some Roman legionaries had stopped and with brusque kindness asked him if he had any relatives they could take him to. They had addressed him in pidgin-Aramaic and had been surprised when he replied in a strangely accented Latin that was purer than the language they spoke themselves.

They asked him if he was a rabbi or a scholar. He told them he was neither.

The officer of the legionaries had offered him some dried meat and wine. He had eaten the meat and asked for water. They gave it to him.

The men were part of a patrol that passed this way once a month. They were stocky, brown-faced men, with hard, clean-shaven faces. They were dressed in stained leather kilts and breastplates and sandals and had iron helmets on their heads, scabbarded short swords at their hips.

Even as they stood around him in the evening sunlight they did not seem relaxed. The officer, softer-voiced than his men but otherwise much like them save that he wore a metal breastplate and a long cloak and a plume in his helmet, asked the madman what his name was.

For a moment the madman had paused, his mouth opening and closing, as if he could not remember what he was called.

'Karl,' he said at length, doubtfully. It was more a suggestion than a statement.

'Sounds almost like a Roman name,' said one of the legionaries.

'Or Greek, maybe,' said another. 'There are a lot of Greeks round here.'

'Are you a citizen?' the officer asked.

But the madman's mind was evidently wandering. He looked away from them, muttering to himself.

All at once, he looked back at them and said: 'Nazareth. Where is Nazareth?'

'That way.' The officer pointed along the road that cut between the hills.

The madman nodded as if satisfied.

'Karl... Karl... Carlus... I don't know...' The officer reached out and took the madman's chin in his hand, looking into his eyes. 'Are you a Jew?'

This seemed to startle the madman.

He sprang to his feet and tried to push through the circle of soldiers. They let him through, laughing. He was a harmless madman.

They watched him run down the road.

'One of their prophets, perhaps,' said the officer, walking towards his horse. The country was full of them. Every other man you met claimed to be spreading the message of their god. They didn't make trouble and religion actually seemed to keep their minds off rebellion.

We should be grateful, thought the officer.

His men were still laughing.

They began to march down the road in the opposite direction to the one the madman had taken.

★

Later he fell in with a group of people as emaciated as himself. They were on an obscure pilgrimage to a town he had never heard of. Like the Essenes, their sect demanded a strict return to the Mosaic law, but they were vague on other matters, save for some idea that King David would be sent by God to them to help them drive out the Romans and conquer Egypt, a country which they somehow identified with Rome and with Babylon.

They treated him as an equal.

He travelled with them for several days. Then, one night as they camped by the side of the road, a dozen horsemen in armour and livery much more resplendent than that of the Romans came galloping by, knocking over cooking pots and riding through the fires.

'Herod's soldiers!' one of the sect cried.

Women were screaming and men were running into the night. Soon most of them had disappeared and only two women and the madman were left.

The leader of the soldiers had a dark, handsome face and a thick, oiled beard. He pulled the madman up to his knees by his hair and spat in his face.

'Are you one of these rebels we've been hearing so much about?'

The madman muttered, but shook his head.

The soldiers cuffed him. He was so weak that he fell instantly to the ground.

The soldier shrugged. 'He's no threat. There are no arms here. We've been misled.'

He looked calculatingly at the women for a moment and then turned to his men, his eyebrows raised. 'If any of you are hard up enough – you can have them.'

The madman lay on the ground and listened to the cries of the women as they were raped. He felt he should get up and go to their assistance, but he was too weak to move, too afraid of the soldiers. He did not want to be killed. It would mean that he would never achieve his goal.

Herod's soldiers rode away eventually and the members of the sect began to creep back.

'How are the women?' asked the madman.

'They are dead,' someone told him.

Someone else began to chant from the Scriptures, verses about vengeance and righteousness and the punishments of the Lord.

Overwhelmed, the madman crawled away into the darkness.

He left the sect the next morning when he discovered that their route would not take them through Nazareth.

The madman passed through many towns – Philadelphia, Gerasa, Pella and Scythopolis – following the Roman roads.

Of every traveller he met who would stop, he would ask the same question in his outlandish accent: 'Where lies Nazareth?'

In every town he would make sure that he left on the Nazareth road.

In some towns they had given him food. In others they had pelted him with stones and driven him away. In others they had asked for his blessing and he had done what he could, for he wanted the food they would give him, laying hands on them, speaking in his strange tongue.

In Pella he cured a blind woman.

He had crossed the Jordan by the Roman viaduct and continued northwards towards Nazareth.

Although there was no difficulty in getting directions for Nazareth, it became increasingly difficult to force himself towards the town.

He had lost a great deal of blood and had eaten very little on the journey. His manner of travelling was to walk until he collapsed, then lie there until he could go on, or, as had happened increasingly, until someone found him and had given him a little sour wine or bread to revive him.

After the incident with Herod's soldiers, he became warier, and always travelled alone, never identifying himself with any particular sect or group he met.

Sometimes people would ask him, 'Are you the prophet whom we await?'

He would shake his head and say, 'Find Jesus. Find Jesus.'

The white town consisted primarily of double- and single-storeyed houses of stone and clay-brick, built around a market place that was fronted by an ancient, simple synagogue. Outside the synagogue old men, dressed in dark robes and with shawls over their heads, sat and talked.

The town was prosperous and clean, thriving on Roman commerce. Only one or two beggars were in the streets and these were well fed. The streets followed the rise and fall of the hillside on which they were built. They were winding streets, shady and peaceful: country streets.

There was a smell of newly cut timber everywhere in the air, and the sound of carpentry, for the town was chiefly famous for its skilled carpenters. It lay on the edge of the Plain of Jezreel, close to the trade route between Damascus and Egypt, and wagons were always leaving it, laden with the work of the town's craftsmen.

The town was called Nazareth.

Now the madman had found Nazareth.

The townspeople looked at him with curiosity and more than a little suspicion as he staggered into the market square. He could be a wandering prophet or he could be possessed by devils. He could be a beggar or some member of a sect like the Zealots, who were so unpopular these days for the disaster they had brought upon Jerusalem forty years before. The people of Nazareth did not care for rebels or fanatics. They were comfortable, richer than they had ever been before the Romans came.

As the madman passed the knots of people standing by the merchants' stalls, they fell silent until he had gone by.

Women pulled their heavy woollen shawls about their well-fed bodies and men tucked in their cotton robes so that he would not touch them. Normally their instinct would have been to have taxed him with his business in the town, but there was an intensity about his gaze, a quickness and vitality about his face, in spite of his emaciated appearance, that made them treat him with some respect and they kept their distance.

When he reached the centre of the market place, he stopped and looked around him. He seemed slow to notice the people. He blinked and licked his lips.

A woman passed, eyeing him warily. He spoke to her, his voice soft, the words carefully formed.

'Is this Nazareth?'

'It is.' She nodded and increased her pace.

A man was crossing the square. He was dressed in a woollen robe of red and brown stripes. There was a red skull-cap on his curly, black hair. His face was plump and cheerful.

The madman walked across the man's path and stopped him.

'I seek a carpenter.'

'There are many carpenters in Nazareth. It is a town of carpenters! I am a carpenter myself.' The man was good-humoured, patronising. 'Can I help you?'

'Do you know a carpenter called Joseph? A descendant of David. He has a wife called Mary and several children. One is called Jesus.'

The cheerful man screwed his face into a mock frown and scratched the back of his neck. 'I know more than one Joseph. And I know many Marys...' His eyes became reflective then and his lips curved as if in pleasant reminiscence. 'I think I know the one you're looking for. There's a poor fellow in yonder street.' He pointed. 'He has a wife called Mary. Try there. You should soon find him, unless he's delivering his work. Look for a man who never laughs.'

The madman glanced in the direction the man had pointed. As soon as he saw the street, he seemed to forget everything else and began to move mechanically towards it.

In the narrow street the smell of cut timber was even stronger. He walked ankle-deep in wood-shavings.

In Nazareth the heat was less dry than he had become used to. It was more like a fine, English summer's day, a sweet, lazy day...

The madman's heart began to thump.

From every building came a thud of hammers, the scrape of

saws. There were planks of all sizes resting against the pale, shaded walls of the houses and there was hardly room to pass between them.

The madman paused. Fear made him tremble.

Many of the carpenters had their benches just outside their doors. They were carving bowls, operating simple lathes, shaping wood into everything imaginable.

The madman began to move again.

The carpenters looked up as they saw the madman coming down their street. He approached one old carpenter in a leather apron who sat at his bench carving a figurine. The man had grey hair and seemed short-sighted as he peered up at the madman.

'What do you want? I have no money for beggars.'

'I am not a beggar. I am seeking someone who lives in this street.'

'What's his name?'

'Joseph. He has a wife called Mary.'

The old man gestured with his hand that held the half-completed figurine. 'Two houses along on the other side of the street.'

He began to tremble and he began to sweat.

Fool – it's only…

Oh, God…

Probably find they know nothing. This is a coincidence.

Oh, God!

The house the madman came to had very few planks leaning against it and the quality of the timber seemed poorer than the other wood he had seen. The bench near the entrance was warped on one side and the man who sat hunched over it repairing a stool seemed misshapen too.

The madman touched his shoulder and he straightened up. His face was lined and pouched with misery. The eyes were tired and his thin beard had premature streaks of grey. He coughed slightly, perhaps in surprise at being disturbed.

'Are you Joseph?' asked the madman.

'I've no money.'

'I want nothing – just to ask some questions.'

'I'm Joseph. What do you want to know?'

'Have you a son?'

'Several, and daughters, too.'

The madman paused. Joseph looked at him curiously. He seemed to be frightened. It was a new experience for Joseph to find himself the cause of another's fear.

'What's the matter?'

The madman shook his head. 'Nothing.' His voice was hoarse. 'Your wife is called Mary? You are of David's line?'

The man gestured impatiently. 'Yes, yes – for what good either has done me…'

'I wish to meet one of your sons. Have you one called Jesus? Can you tell me where he is?'

'That good-for-nothing. What has he done now?'

'Where is he?'

Joseph's eyes became calculating as he stared at the madman. 'Are you a seer of some kind? Have you come to help my son?'

'I am a prophet of sorts. I believe I can foretell the future.'

Joseph got up with a sigh. 'I haven't much time. I've work to deliver in Nain as soon as possible.'

'Let me see him.'

'You can see him. Come.'

Joseph led the madman through the gateway into the cramped courtyard of the house. It was crowded with pieces of wood, broken furniture and implements, rotting sacks of shavings.

They entered the darkened house.

The madman was breathing heavily.

In the first room, evidently a kitchen, a woman stood by a large clay stove. She was tall and beginning to get fat. Her long black hair was unbound and greasy, falling over large, lustrous eyes that still had the heat of sensuality. She looked the madman over.

'I see you've found another well-paying customer, Joseph,' she said sardonically.

'He's a prophet.'

'Oh, a prophet. And hungry, I suppose. Well, we've no food for beggars or prophets, whatever they choose to call themselves.' She gestured with a wooden spoon at a small figure sitting in the shadow of a corner. 'That useless thing eats enough as it is.' The figure shifted as they spoke.

'He seeks our Jesus,' said Joseph to the woman. 'Perhaps he has come to ease our burden.'

The woman gave the madman a sidelong look and shrugged. She licked her red lips with a fat tongue. 'Maybe you're right. There's something about him...'

'Where is he?' said the madman hoarsely.

The woman put her hands under her large breasts and shifted their position in the rough, brown dress she wore. She rubbed her hand on her stomach and then gave the madman a hooded look. 'Jesus!' she called, not turning.

The figure in the corner stood up.

'That's him,' said the woman with a certain satisfaction.

How?
   It c...
   Jesus!
   I need...
   NO!

The madman frowned, shaking his head rapidly.

'No,' he said. 'No.'

'What do you mean, "no"?' she said querulously. 'I don't care what you do. If you can stop him stealing. He doesn't know any better, but he'll be in real trouble one day, when he steals from someone who doesn't know about him...'

'No...'

The figure was misshapen.

It had a pronounced hunched back and a cast in its left eye. The face was vacant and foolish. There was a little spittle on the lips.

'Jesus?'

It giggled as its name was repeated. It took a crooked, lurching step forward.

'Jesus,' it said. The word was slurred and thick. 'Jesus.'

'That's all he can say,' said the woman. 'He's always been like that.'

'God's judgement,' said Joseph.

'Oh, shut up!' She gave her husband a savage grin.

'What is wrong with him?'

There was a pathetic, desperate note in the madman's voice.

'He's always been like that.' The woman turned back to the stove. 'You can have him if you want him. Take him away with you. Addled inside and outside. I was carrying him when my parents married me off to that half-man...'

'You sow! You shameless...' Joseph stopped as his wife grinned again, daring him to continue. Making some attempt to save his pride, he tried to smile back. 'You had a good story for them, didn't you? The oldest excuse ever! Taken by an angel! Taken by a devil, more likely!'

'He was a devil,' she grinned. 'And he was a man...'

Joseph drooped for a moment, then, as if remembering the fear he had seemed to inspire in the madman earlier, turned to the man and said in a bullying tone, 'What's your business with our son?'

'I wished to talk to him. I...'

'He's no oracle – no seer – we used to think he might be. There are still people in Nazareth who come to him to cure them or tell their fortunes, but he only giggles at them and speaks his name over and over again...'

'Are you sure – there is not – something about him – something you have not noticed?'

'Sure!' Mary snorted emphatically. 'We need money badly enough. If he had any magical powers, we'd know by now.'

Jesus giggled again.

'Jesus,' he said. 'Jesus, Jesus.'

He lurched away into another room.

Joseph ran after him. 'He can't go in there! I won't have him wetting the floor again!'

While Joseph was in the other room, Mary gave the madman another appraising look. 'If you can tell fortunes, you must come and tell mine some time. He'll be leaving tonight for Nain...'

Joseph led the cripple back into the kitchen and made him sit on a stool in the corner. 'Stay there, bastard!'

The madman shook his head. 'It is impossible...'

Had history itself changed?

Was this all the story was based on?

It was impossible...

Joseph appeared to notice the look of agony in the madman's eyes.

'What is it?' he said. 'What do you see? You said you foretold the future. Tell us how we will fare!'

'Not *now*,' said the prophet, turning away. 'How can I? Not now.'

He ran from the dark house and into the sun. He ran down the street with its smell of planed oak, cedar and cypress.

Some of the carpenters looked up, wondering if he was a thief. But they saw he carried nothing.

He ran back to the market place and stopped, looking vacantly about him.

The madman, the prophet, Karl Glogauer, the time-traveller, the neurotic psychiatrist manqué, the searcher for meaning, the masochist, the man with a death-wish and the messiah-complex, the anachronism, made his way through the market place gasping for breath.

He had seen the man he had sought. He had seen Jesus, the son of Mary and Joseph.

He had seen a man he recognised without any doubt as a congenital imbecile.

★

The cheerful man with the red cap was still in the market place, buying cooking pots to give as a wedding present. As the stranger stumbled past, he nodded towards him. 'That's the one.'

'Where's he from?'

'No idea. Not these parts, judging by his accent. I gather he's some relative of old sour-faced Joseph – you know, the one with the wife...'

The man selling pots grinned.

They watched him sink down in the shade by the wall of the synagogue.

'What is he? A religious fanatic? A Zealot or something?' said the man selling pots.

The other shook his head. 'He's got the look of a prophet, hasn't he? But I don't know. Maybe he just fell on hard times where he comes from and decided to seek the help of his relatives...'

'Seek old Joseph's help!' The man laughed.

'Maybe he got driven out of wherever he lived,' said the man with the red cap. 'Who knows? He couldn't have got much joy from Joseph. He wasn't there very long.'

'There's nowhere else for him to go,' said the man selling pots firmly.

He stayed by the wall of the synagogue until nightfall. He began to feel very hungry. Also, for the first time in more than a month, he began to feel lust. It was as if the urge had come to his rescue, as if in lust he could forget the bafflement that filled his head.

He rose slowly and began to make his way back towards the street.

He walked down the street of the carpenters and it was silent now. A few voices could be heard from within the houses, and the bark of a dog.

He reached the house. The bench had gone, and the wood. The gate was barred.

He tapped on it.

There was no reply.

He tapped a little louder, hardly understanding his instinct for discretion.

The gate was opened and her face looked out at him. She gave him a fat, knowing smile.

'Come in,' she said. 'He left for Nain hours ago.'

'I'm hungry,' he said.

'I'll give you something to eat.'

In the kitchen, something stirred in the darkness, but he did not look at it. He hurried through to the next room. A lamp burned there. A ladder led up into an opening in the ceiling.

'Wait here,' she said. 'I'll get food.'

She came and went from the kitchen several times, bringing first water so that he could wash, then a dish of dried meat, bread and a jug of wine.

'It's all we've got,' she said.

She looked into his dark, moody face. He had cleaned the dust from his body and combed out his hair and beard. He looked quite presentable now. But his eyes were withdrawn as he ate the food and he would not look at her directly.

She was breathing heavily now. The lust in her big body was becoming hard to control. She hitched her skirt up to above her calves and spread her legs apart when she sat on the stool near him.

He continued to chew, but now his eyes were on her body.

'Hurry up,' she said.

He finished the food and slowly drank the last of the wine.

Then she was on him, her hands tearing off his rag of a loin-cloth, her fingers on his genitals, her lips on his face, her great body heaving against him.

He gasped and drew up her skirt, driving his fingers into her, rocking against her, rolling her over onto the floor, hastily pushing her legs apart.

She moaned, screamed, snarled, jerked and clawed, then lay still as he continued to thrust into her. But the lust went and he could not finish. He sighed, glancing up suddenly.

The idiot stood in the doorway looking at them, spittle hanging from his chin, a vacant grin on his face.

Part Three

Chapter Thirteen

And the Word was made flesh, and dwelt among us.

(John 1: 14)

E VERY TUESDAY IN the spare room above the Mandala Book-shop, the Jungian discussion group would meet to thrash out difficult points of doctrine and for purposes of group analysis and group therapy.

Glogauer had not organised the group, but he had willingly lent his premises to it. It was a great relief to talk with like-minded people once a week.

An interest in Jung brought them together, but everyone had special interests of his own. Mrs Rita Blen charted the courses of flying saucers, though it was not clear if she actually believed in them or not. Hugh Joyce was convinced that all Jungian arche-types derived from the original race of Lemurians who had perished millennia before. Alan Cheddar, the youngest of the group, was interested in Indian mysticism, and Sandra Peterson, the organ-iser, was a great witchcraft specialist.

James Headington was interested in time. The group's pride, he was Sir James Headington the physicist, wartime inventor, very rich and with all sorts of decorations for his contribution to the Allied victory. He had had the reputation of being a great improviser during the war, but afterwards he had become some-thing of an embarrassment to the War Office. He was barmy, they thought, and what was worse he aired his barminess in public.

Sir James had a thin, aristocratic face (though he had been born in Norwood of middle-class parents), a thin, slightly prissy mouth, a shock of longish white hair and heavy black eyebrows. He wore old-fashioned suits and very bright flower-patterned shirts and ties. Every so often he would tell the other members about the progress he was making with his time machine. They humoured him. Most of them were a little inclined to exaggerate their own experiences connected with their different interests.

One Tuesday evening, after everyone else had left, Headington asked Glogauer if he would like to go out to Banbury and have a look over his laboratory.

'I'm doing all sorts of spectacular experiments at the moment. Sending rabbits through time, that sort of thing. You really must look over the lab.'

'I can't believe it,' Glogauer said. 'You're really able to send things through time?'

'Oh, yes. You're the first I've told about it.'

'I can't believe it!' And he couldn't.

'Come down and have a look for yourself.'

'Why are you telling me?'

'Oh, I don't know. I like you, I suppose.'

Glogauer smiled. 'Well, all right. I will come down. When would be best?'

'Any time you like. Why not come down Friday and stay over the weekend?'

'You're sure you don't mind?'

'Not a bit!'

'I have a girlfriend…'

'Mmm…' Headington looked doubtful. 'I'm not too keen to broadcast this everywhere at the moment…'

'I'll put her off.'

'Good man! Catch the six-ten from Paddington if you can. I'll meet you at the station. See you Friday.'

'See you Friday.'

Glogauer watched him leave and he began to grin. The old boy was probably mad. He probably had a whole lot of expensive electronic junk down there, but it would be fun to have a weekend away from London and see exactly what was going on at Banbury.

★

Headington owned a large old rectory in a village about two miles from Banbury. The laboratory buildings in the grounds were all fairly new.

Headington employed two young men as full-time assistants; they were just leaving as the physicist guided Glogauer into the main building.

As Glogauer had suspected, the place was a clutter of Heath Robinson gadgets, with wires and cables hanging everywhere.

'Here,' said Headington, drawing Glogauer by the arm to a clearer part of the laboratory. On a wide bench stood several black boxes wired together. In the centre of these was another box, of silver grey.

Headington glanced at his watch and studied the dials on the black boxes. 'Now. Let's see.' He adjusted various controls. Then he went to a bank of cages on the other side of the room and removed a twitching white rabbit. He placed the rabbit in the silver box, made a few more adjustments to the controls on the black boxes, then turned a switch that had been screwed to the bench. 'Power,' he said.

Glogauer blinked. The air had seemed to shake for a moment. The silver box was gone.

'Good God!'

Headington chuckled. 'See – off through time!'

'It's vanished,' Glogauer agreed. 'But that doesn't prove it's gone into the future.'

'True. In fact it's gone into the past. Can't get into the future. An impossibility at the moment.'

'Well – I meant it didn't prove that the rabbit's travelling through time.'

'Where else could it have gone? Take my word for it, Glogauer. That rabbit's gone back a hundred years.'

'How do you know?'

'Short-range tests have proved it. I can send something back to a pretty accurately worked-out date. Believe me.'

Glogauer folded his arms across his chest. 'I believe you, Sir James.'

'We're building the big job now. Be able to send a man back.

Only trouble is, the trip's a bit rough at present. Look...' He touched a stud on the nearest black box. Immediately, the silver box was back on the bench. Glogauer touched it. It was quite hot.

'Here.' Headington reached into the box and drew out the rabbit. Its head was bloody and its bones seemed to be broken. It was alive, but evidently in dreadful pain. 'See what I mean?' said Headington. 'Poor little thing.'

Glogauer turned away.

Back in the study Headington talked about his experiments, but he assumed that Glogauer was familiar with the language of physics and Glogauer was too proud to admit he knew next to nothing about physics, so he sat in his chair for several hours, nodding intelligently while Headington went on enthusiastically.

Headington showed him to his bedroom later. It was an oak-panelled room with a wide, comfortable modern bed.

'Sleep well,' said Headington.

That night, Glogauer was awakened and saw a figure seated on the edge of his bed. It was Headington and he was completely naked. He had his hand on Karl's shoulder.

'I don't suppose...' began Headington.

Glogauer shook his head. 'Sorry, Sir James.'

'Ah well,' said Headington. 'Ah well.'

Immediately he had left, Glogauer began to masturbate.

Headington had telephoned him several days later to ask if he'd like to make another trip to Banbury, but Glogauer had refused politely.

'We're ironing out some of the minor problems,' Headington had told him. 'For instance, we've decided on the best way to protect the passenger. Neither of my lads will volunteer to be it, though. You're not interested, are you, Glogauer?'

'No,' Glogauer said. 'Sorry, Sir James.'

During the next few weeks, Glogauer became disturbed. Monica came less frequently to see him and, when she did, she seemed to have no enthusiasm for love-making of any sort.

One night he lost his temper and began raving at her.

'What's the matter with you? You're as cold as a barrel of ice-cream!'

She stood half an hour of this before she said wearily, 'Well, I had to tell you sometime. If you must know, I'm having an affair with somebody.'

'What?' He calmed immediately. 'I don't believe it.' He had always been so confident that nobody else would be attracted to her. He almost asked her who would have her, but changed his mind.

'Who is he?' he said at last.

'She,' said Monica. 'It's a girl at the hospital. It makes a change.'

'Oh, Jesus!'

Monica sighed. 'It's a relief, really. I don't get an awful lot out of it – but I've got so sick of your emotions, Karl. Sick and tired.'

'Then why don't you leave me altogether? What sort of a compromise is this?'

'I suppose I can't give up hope,' said Monica. 'I still think there's something in you worth working on. I'm a fool, I suppose.'

'What are you trying to do to me?' He had become hysterical. 'What – what's...? You've betrayed me!'

'See what I mean. It's not a betrayal, Karl – it's a bloody holiday.'

'Then you'd better make it permanent,' he said wildly, going over to her clothes and throwing them at her. 'Fuck off, you bitch!'

She got up with a weary resigned expression and began to dress.

When she was ready she opened the door. He was crying on the bed.

'Cheerio, Karl.'

'Fuck off!'

The door closed.

'You bitch! Oh, you bitch!'

The next morning, he telephoned Sir James Headington.

'I've changed my mind,' he said. 'I'll do what you want me to do. I'll be your subject. There's only one condition.'

'What's that?'

'I want to choose the time and place I go to.'

'Fair enough.'

A week later they were on board a privately chartered ship bound for the Middle East. A week after that he left 1970 and arrived in AD 28.

Chapter Fourteen

THE SYNAGOGUE WAS cool and quiet with a subtle scent of incense. Dressed in the clean white robe Mary had given him when he had left early that morning, he let the rabbis guide him into the courtyard. They, like the townspeople, did not know what to make of him, but they were sure that it was not a devil that possessed him.

From time to time he would look down at his body and touch it as if in surprise, or he would finger the robe, puzzled. He had almost forgotten Mary.

'All men have a messiah-complex, Karl,' Monica had said once.

The memories were less complete now – if they were memories at all. He was becoming confused.

'There were dozens of messiahs in Galilee at the time. That Jesus should have been the one to carry the myth and the philosophy was a coincidence of history...'

'There must have been more to it than that, Monica.'

It was the rabbis' custom to give shelter to many of the roaming prophets who were now everywhere in Galilee, as long as they were not members of the outlawed sect.

This one was stranger than the rest. His face was immobile most of the time and his body was still, but tears frequently coursed down his cheeks. They had never seen such agony in a man's eyes before.

'Science can say how, but it never asks why,' he had told Monica. 'It can't answer.'

'Who wants to know?' she replied.

'I do.'

'Well, you'll never find out, will you?'

Bitch! Betrayer! Bastard!

Why did they always let him down?

'Be seated, my son,' said the rabbi. 'What do you wish to ask of us?'

'Where is Christ?' he said.

They did not understand the language.

'Is it Greek?' asked one, but another shook his head.

Kyrios: The Lord.

Adonai: The Lord.

Where was the Lord?

He frowned, looking vaguely about him.

'I must rest,' he said in their language.

'Where are you from?'

He could not think what to answer.

'Where are you from?' a rabbi repeated.

At length he murmured, *'Ha-Olam Hab-Bah…'*

They looked at one another. *'Ha-Olam Hab-Bah,'* they said.

Ha-Olam Hab-Bah; Ha-Olam Haz-Zeh: The world to come and the world that is.

'Do you bring us a message?' said one of the rabbis. This prophet was so different. So strange, one could almost believe that he was a true prophet. 'A message?'

'I do not know,' said the prophet hoarsely. 'I must rest. I am dirty. I have sinned.'

'Come. We will give you food and a place to sleep. We will show you where to bathe and where to pray.'

Servants brought hot water and he cleansed his body. They trimmed his beard and hair and cut his nails.

Then, in the cell that the rabbis had set aside for their visitor, they brought rich food which he found it difficult to eat. And the bed with its straw-stuffed mattress was too soft for him. He was not used to it. But he had had no real rest at Joseph's house and he lay down on it.

He slept badly, shouting as he dreamed, and, outside the room, the rabbis listened, but could understand little of what he said.

'Of all things you should study, Karl, I should have thought Aramaic would be the last! No wonder you...'

My devil, my temptress, my desire, my cross, my love, my lust, my need, my food, my anchor, my master, my slave, my flesh, my satisfaction, my destroyer.

Ah, for all the loving days that might have been if I had been strong; for Eva and those who did not want me for my weaknesses; for all the rewards granted to the brave, for all the realities given to the strong, I yearn. This is the final irony.

The formal irony, inevitable and just.

And I am not satisfied.

Karl Glogauer stayed in the synagogue for several weeks. He would spend most of his time reading in the library, searching through the long scrolls for some answer to his dilemma. The words of the Testaments, in many cases capable of a dozen interpretations, only confused him further. There was nothing to grasp, nothing to tell him what had gone wrong.

This is a comedy. Is this what I deserve? Is there no hope? No solution?

The rabbis kept their distance for the most part. They had accepted him as a holy man. They were proud to have him in their synagogue. They were sure that he was one of the special chosen of God and they waited patiently for him to speak to them.

But the prophet said little, muttering only to himself in snatches of their own language and snatches of the incomprehensible language he often used, even when he addressed them directly.

In Nazareth, the townsfolk talked of little else but the mysterious prophet in the synagogue. They knew he was a relative of Joseph and Joseph was now proud to acknowledge the fact. They knew that Joseph was of the line of David, whatever the sour-faced carpenter was otherwise. So therefore the prophet was of the line of David. An important sign, everyone agreed.

They would ask questions of the rabbis but the wise men would tell them nothing, save that they should go about their business, that there were things they were not yet meant to know. In this way, as priests had always done, they avoided questions they could not answer while at the same time appearing to have much more knowledge than they actually possessed.

Then, one sabbath, he appeared in the public part of the synagogue and took his place with the others who had come to worship.

The man who was reading from the scroll on his left stumbled over the words, glancing at the prophet from the corner of his eye.

The prophet sat and listened, his expression remote.

The chief rabbi looked uncertainly at him, then signed that the scroll should be passed to the prophet. This was done hesitantly by a boy who placed the scroll in the prophet's hands.

The prophet looked at the words for a long time and it seemed that he would refuse to read, for he looked startled. Then he straightened his shoulders and began to read in a clear voice, almost without trace of his usual accent. He read from the book of Esaias.

The people listened with close attention.

The Spirit of the Lord is upon me, because he hath anointed me to preach the gospel to the poor; he hath sent me to heal the broken-hearted, to preach deliverance to the captives, and recovering of sight to the blind, to set at liberty them that are bruised, to preach the acceptable year of the Lord. And he closed the book, and gave it again

to the minister, and sat down. And the eyes of all of them that were
in the synagogue were fastened on him.

(Luke 4: 18–20)

Glogauer did not thereafter resume his study of the Testaments, but took to walking about the streets and talking to the people. They would be respectful, asking his advice on all manner of things, and he would do his best to give them good advice.

Not since his first weeks with Eva had he felt like this.

He resolved not to lose it a second time.

When at first they asked him to lay hands on the sick, he was reluctant and refused, but once, with what seemed to be an obvious case of hysterical blindness, judging from what the relatives told him, he did lay his hands on the woman's eyes and her blindness left her.

In spite of himself, Glogauer returned to his cell in the synagogue excited. There were so many examples of hysterical conditions of all kinds here.

Perhaps it was the creation of the times, he could not tell. At last he dismissed the thoughts. He would worry about them later.

The next day he saw Mary crossing the market place. She led her bastard son by his coat.

Glogauer turned hurriedly and went back into the synagogue.

Chapter Fifteen

THEY FOLLOWED HIM now, as he walked away from Nazareth towards the Lake of Galilee. He was dressed in the fresh white linen robe they had given him and he moved with wonderful dignity and grace; a great leader, a great prophet; but though they thought he led them, they, in fact, drove him before them.

To those that asked on the way they said, 'He is our messiah.' And there were already rumours of many miracles.

My redemption, my rôle, my destiny. In overcoming one temptation I must first succumb to another; cowardice and pride. Living a lie to create the truth. I have betrayed so many who have betrayed me because I betrayed myself.

But Monica would approve of my pragmatism now…

When he saw the sick, he pitied them and tried to do what he could because they expected something of him. Many he could do nothing for, but others, obviously with easily remedied psychosomatic conditions, he could help. They believed in his power more strongly than they believed in their sickness. So he cured them.

When he came to Capernaum some fifty people followed him into the streets of the city. It was already known that he was in some way associated with John the Baptist, who enjoyed considerable prestige in Galilee and had been declared a true prophet by many Pharisees. Yet this man had a power greater, in some ways, than John's. He was not the orator that the Baptist was, but he had worked miracles.

Capernaum was a sprawling town beside the crystal lake of Galilee, its houses separated by large market gardens. Fishing boats were moored at the white quayside, as well as trading ships that plied the lakeside towns.

Though the green hills came down from all sides of the lake, Capernaum itself was built on flat ground, sheltered by the hills. It was a quiet town and, like most others in Galilee, had a large population of gentiles. Greek, Roman and Egyptian traders walked its streets and many had permanent homes there. There was a prosperous middle class of merchants, artisans and ship-owners as well as doctors, lawyers and scholars, for Capernaum was on the borders of the provinces of Galilee, Trachonitis and Syria and, though a comparatively small town, was a useful junction for trade and travel.

The strange, mad prophet in his swirling linen robes, followed by the heterogeneous crowd that was primarily composed of poor folk, but also could be seen to contain men of some distinction, swept into Capernaum.

The news had spread that the man really could foretell the future, that he had already predicted the arrest of John by Herod Antipas and soon after Herod had imprisoned the Baptist at Peraea.

That was what impressed them. He did not make his predictions in general terms, using vague words the way other prophets did. He spoke of things that were to happen in the near future and he spoke of them in detail.

None, at this point, knew his name. That gave him an added mystery, an added stature. He was simply the prophet from Nazareth, or the Nazarene.

Some said he was a relative, perhaps the son, of a carpenter in Nazareth but this could be because the written words for 'son of a carpenter' and 'magus' were almost the same and the confusion had come about in this way.

There was even a very faint rumour that his name was Jesus. The name had been used once or twice, but when they asked him if that was, indeed, his name, he denied it or else, in his abstracted way, refused to answer at all.

His actual preaching tended to lack the fire and point of John's and many of his references seemed particularly oblique, even to the religious men and the scholars whose curiosity brought them to listen to him.

This man spoke gently, rather vaguely, and smiled often. He spoke of God in a strange way, too, and he appeared to be connected, as John was, with the Essenes, for he preached against the accumulation of personal wealth and spoke of mankind as a brotherhood, as they did.

But it was the miracles that they watched for as he was guided to the graceful synagogue of Capernaum.

No prophet before him had healed the sick and seemed to understand the troubles that people rarely spoke of. It was his sympathy that they responded to, rather than the words he spoke.

Yet sometimes he would become withdrawn and refuse to speak, would become lost in his own thoughts, and some would notice how tortured his eyes seemed, and they would leave him, believing him to be communicating with God.

These periods grew less lengthy and he would spend more time with the sick and the miserable, doing what he could for them, and even the wise and the rich in Capernaum began to respect him.

Perhaps the greatest change in him was that for the first time in his life Karl Glogauer had forgotten about Karl Glogauer. For the first time in his life he was doing what he had always considered himself too weak to do, and at the same time fulfilling his largest ambition, to achieve what he had hoped to achieve before he gave up psychiatry.

There was something more, something that he recognised instinctively rather than intellectually. He now had the opportunity to find at the same time both redemption and confirmation for his life up to the moment he had fled from John the Baptist in the desert.

But it was not his own life he would be leading now. He was bringing a myth to life, a generation before that myth would be born. He was completing a certain kind of psychic circuit. He told himself that he was not changing history; he was merely giving history more substance.

Since he had never been able to bear to think that Jesus had been nothing more than a myth, it became a duty to himself to make Jesus a physical reality rather than the creation of a process of mythogenesis. Why did it matter? he wondered; but he would be quick to dismiss the question, for such questions confused him, seemed to offer a trap, an escape and the possibility, once again, of self-betrayal.

So he spoke in the synagogues and he spoke of a gentler God than most of them had heard of, and where he could remember them, he told them parables.

And gradually the need to justify intellectually what he was doing faded and his sense of identity grew increasingly more tenuous and was replaced by a different sense of identity, in which he would give greater and greater substance to the rôle he had chosen. It was an archetypal rôle in all senses, a rôle to appeal to a disciple of Jung. It was a rôle that went beyond mere imitation. It was a rôle that he must now play out to the very last detail.

Karl Glogauer had discovered the reality he had been seeking. That was not to say he did not still have doubts.

And in the synagogue there was a man, which had a spirit of an unclean devil, and cried out with a loud voice, saying, Let us alone; what have we to do with thee, thou Jesus of Nazareth? art thou come to destroy us? I know thee who thou art; the Holy One of God. And Jesus rebuked him, saying, Hold thy peace, and come out of him. And when the devil had thrown him in the midst, he came out of him, and hurt him not. And they were all amazed, and spake among themselves, saying, What a word is this! for with authority and power he commandeth the unclean spirits, and they come out. And the fame of him went out into every place of the country round about.

(Luke 4: 33–37)

Chapter Sixteen

*I know that my redeemer liveth, and that he shall stand at the
latter day upon the earth.*

(Job 19: 25)

O felix culpa, quae talem ac tantum meruit habere Redemptorem.
(Missal – *Exultet* on Holy Saturday)

'MASS HALLUCINATION. MIRACLES, flying saucers, ghosts,
the beast from the id, it's all the same,' Monica had said.
'Very likely,' he had replied. 'But *why* did they see them?'
'Because they wanted to.'
'Why did they want to?'
'Because they were afraid.'
'You think that's all there is to it?'
'Isn't it enough?'

When he left Capernaum for the first time, many more people
accompanied him.

It had become impractical to stay in the town, for its business
had been brought almost to a standstill by the crowds that sought
to see him work his simple miracles.

So he spoke to them in the spaces between the towns, from
hillsides and on the banks of rivers.

He talked with intelligent, literate men who appeared to have
something in common with him. Among these were the owners
of fishing fleets – Simon, James and John and others. Another was
a doctor, another a civil servant who had first heard him speak in
Capernaum.

'There must be twelve,' he said to them one day, and he smiled. 'There must be a zodiac.'

And he picked them out by their names. 'Is there a man here called Peter? Is there one called Judas?'

And when he had picked them, he asked the others to go away for a while, for he wished to talk to the twelve alone.

It must be as exact as I can remember. There will be difficulties, discrepancies, but I must at least supply the basic structure.

He was not careful in what he said, people noticed. He was even more specific in his attacks and his examples than John the Baptist. Few prophets were as brave; few offered such confidence.

Many of his ideas were strange. Many of the things he talked about were unfamiliar to them. Some Pharisees thought he blasphemed.

Occasionally someone would attempt to warn him, suggest that for the sake of his cause he modify some of his pronouncements, but he would smile and shake his head. 'No. I must say what I must say. It is already decided.'

One day he met a man he recognised as an Essene from the colony near Machaerus.

'John would speak with you,' said the Essene.

'Is John not dead yet?' he asked the man.

'He is confined at Paraea. I would think Herod is too frightened to kill him. He lets John walk about within the walls and gardens of the palace, lets him speak with his men, but John fears that Herod will find the courage soon to have him stoned or decapitated. He needs your help.'

'How can I help him? He is to die. There is no hope for him.'

The Essene looked uncomprehendingly into the mad eyes of the prophet.

'But, master, there is no-one else who can help him.'

'He must not be helped. He must die.'

'He told me, if you refused at first, to say that you failed him once, do not fail him now.'

'I am not failing him. I am redeeming my failure now. I have done all that I should have done. I have healed the sick and preached to the poor.'

'I did not know he wished this. Now he needs help, master. You could save his life. You are powerful and the people listen to your words. Herod could not refuse you.'

The prophet drew the Essene away from the twelve.

'His life cannot be saved.'

'Is it God's will?'

The prophet paused and looked down at the ground.

'John must die.'

'Master – is it God's will?'

The prophet looked up and spoke solemnly. 'If I am God, then it is God's will.'

Hopelessly, the Essene turned and began to walk away from the prophet.

The prophet sighed, remembering the Baptist and how he had liked him. Doubtless John had been chiefly responsible for saving his life. But there was nothing he could do. John the Baptist was ordained to die.

He moved on, with his following, through Galilee. Apart from his twelve educated men, the rest who followed him were still primarily poor people. To them he offered their only hope of good fortune. Many were those who had been ready to follow John against the Romans. But now John was imprisoned.

Perhaps this man would lead them in revolt, to loot the riches of Jerusalem and Jericho and Caesarea?

Tired and hungry, their eyes glazed by the burning sun, they followed the man in the white robe. They needed to hope and they found reasons for their hope. They saw him work greater miracles.

Once he preached to them from a boat, as was often his custom, and as he walked back to the shore through the shallows, it seemed to them that he walked over the water.

All through Galilee in the autumn they wandered, hearing from everyone the news of John's beheading. Despair at the Baptist's death turned to renewed hope in this fresh prophet who had known him.

In Caesarea they were driven from the city by Roman guards used to the wild men with their prophecies who roamed the rural districts.

They were banned from other cities as the prophet's fame grew. Not only the Roman authorities, but the Jewish ones as well seemed unwilling to tolerate the new prophet as they had tolerated John. The political climate was changing.

It became hard to get food. They lived on what they could find, hungering like starved animals.

Karl Glogauer, witch-doctor, psychiatrist, hypnotist, messiah, taught them how to pretend to eat and take their minds off their hunger.

The Pharisees also with the Sadducees came, and tempting desired him that he would shew them a sign from heaven. He answered and said unto them, When it is evening, ye say, It will be fair weather: for the sky is red. And in the morning, It will be foul weather to day: for the sky is red and lowring. O ye hypocrites, ye can discern the face of the sky; but can ye not discern the signs of the times?

(Matthew 16: 1–3)

'You must be more careful. You will be stoned. They will kill you.'

'They will not stone me.'

'That is the law.'

'It is not my fate.'

'Do you not fear death?'

'It is not the greatest of my fears.'

★

I fear my own ghost. I fear that the dream will end. I fear...

But I am not lonely now.

Sometimes his conviction in his chosen role wavered and those that followed him would be disturbed when he contradicted himself.

Often now they called him the name they had heard, Jesus the Nazarene.

Most of the time he did not stop them from using the name, but at others he became angry and cried peculiar, guttural words.

'Karl Glogauer! Karl Glogauer!'

And they said, Behold, he speaks with the voice of Adonai.

'Call me not by that name!' he would shout, and they would become disturbed and leave him by himself until his anger had subsided. Usually, then, he would seek them out, as if anxious for their company.

I fear my own ghost. I fear the lonely Glogauer.

They noticed that he did not like to see his own reflection and they said that he was modest and sought to emulate him.

When the weather changed and the winter came, they went back to Capernaum, which had become a stronghold of his followers.

In Capernaum he waited the winter through talking to all who would listen, and most of his words concerned prophecies.

Many of these prophecies concerned himself and the fates of those that followed him.

Then charged he his disciples that they should tell no man that he was Jesus the Christ. From that time forth began Jesus to shew unto his disciples, how that he must go unto Jerusalem, and suffer many things of the elders and chief priests and scribes, and be killed, and be raised again the third day.

(Matthew 16: 20–21)

They were watching television at her flat. Monica was eating an apple. It was between six and seven on a warm Sunday evening. Monica gestured at the screen with her half-eaten apple.

'Look at that nonsense,' she said. 'You can't honestly tell me it means anything to you.'

The programme was a religious one, about a pop-opera in a Hampstead church. The opera told the story of the crucifixion.

'Pop-groups in the pulpit,' she said. 'What a comedown.'

He didn't reply. The programme seemed obscene to him, in an obscure way. He couldn't argue with her.

'God's corpse is really beginning to rot now,' she jeered. 'Whew! What a stink!'

'Turn it off, then…'

'What's the pop-group called? The Maggots?'

'Very funny. I'll turn it off, shall I?'

'No, I want to watch. It's amusing.'

'Oh, turn it off!'

'Imitation of Christ!' she snorted. 'It's a bloody caricature.'

A negro singer, who was playing Christ and singing flat to a banal accompaniment, began to drone out lifeless lyrics about the brotherhood of man.

'If he sounded like that, no wonder they nailed him up,' said Monica.

He reached forward and switched the picture off.

'I was enjoying it,' she said in mock disappointment. 'It was a lovely swan-song.'

Later, she said with a trace of affection that worried him, 'You old fogey. What a pity. You could have been John Wesley or Calvin or someone. You can't be a messiah these days, not in your terms. There's nobody to listen.'

Chapter Seventeen

THE PROPHET WAS living in the house of a man called Simon, though the prophet preferred to call him Peter. Simon was grateful to the prophet because he had cured his wife of a complaint which she had suffered from for some time. It had been a mysterious illness, but the prophet had cured her almost effortlessly.

There were a great many strangers in Capernaum at that time, many of them coming to see the prophet. Simon warned him that some were known agents of the Romans or the hostile Pharisees. Many of the Pharisees had not, on the whole, been antipathetic towards the prophet, though they distrusted the talk of miracles they had heard. However, the whole political atmosphere was disturbed and the Roman occupation force, from Pilate, through his officers, down to the troops, was tense, expecting an outbreak but unable to see any really tangible signs that one was coming.

An abnormally abstemious man, Pilate poured water into the small measure of wine at the bottom of the cup and considered his position.

He hoped for trouble on a large scale.

If some sort of rebel band, like the Zealots, attacked Jerusalem, it would prove to Tiberius that he had, against all Pilate's advice, been too lenient with the Jews over the matter of the votive shields. Pilate would be vindicated and his power over the Jews increased. Perhaps then he could start to put through some real policies. At present he was on bad terms with all the tetrarchs of the provinces – particularly with the unstable Herod Antipas who had seemed at one time his only supporter.

Aside from the political situation, his own domestic situation was upset in that his neurotic wife was having her nightmares again and was demanding far more attention than he could afford to give her.

There might be a possibility, he thought, of provoking an incident, but he would have to be careful that Tiberius never learnt of it.

He wondered if this new prophet might provide a focus. So far the man had proved a bit disappointing. He had done nothing against the laws of either the Jews or the Romans, though he had been a trifle scathing about the established priesthood. Still, nobody ever worried about that – it was common to attack the priesthood in general. The priests themselves were too complacent most of the time to pay much attention to attacks. There was no law that forbade a man to claim he was a messiah, as some said this one had done, and he was hardly, at this stage, inciting the people to revolt – rather the contrary. Also one couldn't arrest a man because some of his followers were ex-followers of John the Baptist. The whole Baptist business had been mishandled when Herod had panicked.

Looking through the window of his chamber, with a view of the minarets and spires of Jerusalem, Pilate considered the information his agents had brought him.

Soon after the festival that the Romans called Saturnalia, the prophet and his followers left Capernaum again and began to travel through the country.

There were fewer miracles now that the hot weather had passed, but his prophecies were eagerly sought. He warned them of all the mistakes that would be made in the future, and of all the crimes that would be committed in his name, and he begged them to think before they acted in the name of Christ.

Through Galilee he wandered, and through Samaria, following the good Roman roads towards Jerusalem.

The time of the Passover was coming close now.

I have done all that I could think of to do. I have worked miracles, I have preached, I have chosen my disciples. But all this had been easy, because I have been what the people demanded. I am their creation.

Have I done enough? Has the course been set irrevocably?

We shall know soon.

In Jerusalem, the Roman officials discussed the coming festival. It was always a time of the worst disturbances. There had been riots before during the Feast of the Passover, and doubtless there would be trouble of some kind this year, too.

Pilate asked the Pharisees to come to see him. When they arrived, he spoke to them as ingratiatingly as possible, asking for their co-operation.

The Pharisees said they would do what they could, but they could not help it if the people acted foolishly.

Pilate was pleased. He had been seen by the others to be trying to avert trouble. If it came now, he could not be blamed.

'You see,' he said to the other officials. 'What can you do with them?'

'We'll get as many troops as we can recalled to Jerusalem as soon as possible,' said his second in command. 'But we're already spread a bit thin.'

'We must do our best,' said Pilate.

When they had gone, Pilate sent for his agents. They told him that the new prophet was on his way.

Pilate rubbed his chin.

'He seems harmless enough,' said one of the men.

'He might be harmless now,' said Pilate, 'but if he reaches Jerusalem during the Passover, he might not be so harmless.'

Two weeks before the Feast of the Passover, the prophet reached the town of Bethany near Jerusalem. Some of his Galilean followers had friends in Bethany and these friends were more than willing to shelter the man they had heard of from other pilgrims on their way to Jerusalem and the Great Temple.

The reason they had come to Bethany was that the prophet had become disturbed by the number of people following him.

'There are too many,' he had said to Simon. 'Too many, Peter.'

His face was haggard now. His eyes were set deeper into their sockets and he said little.

Sometimes he would look around him vaguely, as if unsure where he was.

News came to the house in Bethany that Roman agents had been making enquiries about him. It did not disturb him. On the contrary, he nodded thoughtfully, as if satisfied.

'Pilate is said to be looking for a scapegoat,' warned John.

'Then he shall have one,' replied the prophet.

Once he walked with two of his followers across country to look at Jerusalem. The bright yellow walls of the city looked splendid in the afternoon light. The towers and tall buildings, many of them decorated in mosaic reds, blues and yellows, could be seen from several miles away.

The prophet turned back towards Bethany.

There it is and I am afraid. Afraid of death and afraid of blasphemy.

But there is no other way. There is no sure manner to accomplish this save to live it through.

'When shall we go into Jerusalem?' one of his followers asked him.

'Not yet,' said Glogauer. His shoulders were hunched and he grasped his chest with his arms and hands as if cold.

Two days before the Feast of the Passover in Jerusalem, the prophet took his men towards the Mount of Olives and a suburb of Jerusalem that was built on the slopes of the mount and called Bethphage.

'Get me a donkey,' he told them. 'A colt. I must fulfil the prophecy now.'

'Then all will know you are the messiah,' said Andrew.

'Yes.'

The prophet sighed.

★

This fear is not the same. It is more the fear of an actor about to play his final, most dramatic scene…

There was cold sweat on the prophet's lip. He wiped it off.

In the poor light he peered at the men around him. He was still uncertain of some of their faces. He had been interested only in their names and their number. There were ten here. The other two were looking for the donkey.

There was a light, warm breeze blowing. They stood on the grassy slope of the Mount of Olives, looking towards Jerusalem and the Great Temple which lay below.

'Judas?' said Glogauer hesitantly.

There was one called Judas.

'Yes, master,' he said. He was tall and good-looking with curly red hair and neurotic, intelligent eyes. Glogauer believed he was an epileptic.

Glogauer looked thoughtfully at Judas Iscariot. 'I will want you to help me later,' he said, 'when we have entered Jerusalem.'

'How, master?'

'You must take a message to the Romans.'

'The Romans?' Judas looked troubled. 'Why?'

'It must be the Romans. It can't be the Jews. They would use stones or a stake or an axe. I'll tell you more when the time comes.'

The sky was dark now, and the stars were out over the Mount of Olives. It had become cold. Glogauer shivered.

Chapter Eighteen

Rejoice greatly O daughter of Zion,
Shout, O daughter of Jerusalem:
Behold, thy King cometh unto thee!
He is just and having salvation;
Lowly and riding upon an ass,
And upon a colt, the foal of an ass.
(Zechariah 9: 9)

'*O*SHA'NA! OSHA'NA! OSHA'NA!'

As Glogauer rode the donkey into the city, his followers ran ahead, throwing down palm branches. On both sides of the street were crowds, forewarned by the followers of his coming.

Now the prophet could be seen to be fulfilling the prophecies of the ancient prophets and many more believed in him, believed that he had come, in Adonai's name, to lead them against the Romans. Even now, possibly, he was on his way to Pilate's house to confront the procurator.

'*Osha'na! Osha'na!*'

Glogauer looked around distractedly. The back of the donkey, though softened by the coats of his followers, was uncomfortable. He swayed and clung to the beast's mane. He heard the words, but could not make them out clearly.

'*Osha'na! Osha'na!*'

It sounded like 'Hosanna' at first, before he realised that they were shouting the Aramaic for 'Free us'.

'Free us! Free us!'

John had planned to rise in arms against the Romans this Passover. Many had expected to take part in the rebellion.

They believed that he was taking John's place as a rebel leader.

'No,' he muttered at them as he looked around at their expectant faces. 'No. I am the messiah. I cannot free you. I can't…'

Their faith was unfounded, but they did not hear him above their own shouts.

Karl Glogauer entered Christ and Christ entered Jerusalem. The story was approaching its climax.

'Osha'na!'

It was not in the story. He could not help them.

It was his flesh.

It was his flesh being given away piece by piece to whoever desired it. It no longer belonged to him.

> Verily, verily, I say unto you, that one of you shall betray me. Then the disciples looked one on another, doubting of whom he spake. Now there was leaning on Jesus' bosom one of his disciples, whom Jesus loved. Simon Peter therefore beckoned to him, that he should ask who it should be of whom he spake. He then lying on Jesus' breast saith unto him, Lord, who is it? Jesus answered, He it is, to whom I shall give a sop, when I have dipped it. And when he had dipped the sop, he gave it to Judas Iscariot, the son of Simon. And after the sop Satan entered into him. Then said Jesus unto him, That thou doest, do quickly.
>
> (John 13: 21–27)

Judas Iscariot frowned with some uncertainty as he left the room and went out into the crowded street, making his way towards the governor's palace. Doubtless he was to perform a part in a plan to deceive the Romans and have the people rise up in Jesus' defence, but he thought the scheme foolhardy. The mood amongst the jostling men, women and children in the streets was tense. Many more Roman soldiers than usual patrolled the city.

'But they have no cause to arrest you, Lord,' he had said to the prophet.

'I will give them cause,' the prophet had replied.

★

There had been no other way to organise it.

He did not think it would matter. The chroniclers would rearrange it.

Pilate was a stout man in spite of eating and drinking little. His mouth was self-indulgent and his eyes were large and shallow.

He looked disdainfully at the Jew.

'We do not pay informers whose information is proved to be false,' he warned.

'I do not seek money, Lord,' said Judas, feigning the ingratiating manner that the Romans seemed to expect of the Jews. 'I am a loyal subject of the emperor.'

'Who is this rebel?'

'Jesus of Nazareth, lord. He entered the city today…'

'I know. I saw him. But I heard he preached of peace and obeying the law.'

'To deceive you, lord. But today he has betrayed himself, angering the Pharisees, speaking against the Romans. He has revealed his true intentions.'

Pilate frowned. It was likely. It smacked of the kind of deceit he had grown to anticipate in these soft-spoken people.

'Have you proof?'

'There are a hundred witnesses.'

'Witnesses have poor memories,' said Pilate with some feeling. 'How do we identify them?'

'Then I will testify to his guilt. I am one of his lieutenants.'

It seemed too good to be true. Pilate pursed his lips. He could not afford to offend the Pharisees at this moment. They had given him enough trouble. Caiaphas, in particular, would be quick to cry 'injustice' if he arrested the man.

'You say he has offended the priests?'

'He claims to be the rightful king of the Jews, the descendant of David,' said Judas, repeating what his master had told him to say.

'Does he?' Pilate looked thoughtfully out of the window.

'As for the Pharisees, lord…'

'What of them?'

'They would see him dead. I have it on good authority. Certain of the Pharisees who disagree with the majority tried to warn him to flee the city, but he refused.'

Pilate nodded. His eyes were hooded as he considered this information. The Pharisees might hate the prophet, but they would be quick to make political capital out of his arrest.

'The Pharisees want him taken into custody,' Judas continued. 'The people flock to listen to the prophet and today many of them rioted in the Temple in his name.'

'That was him, was it?' It was true that some half a dozen people had attacked the money-changers in the Temple and tried to rob them.

'Ask those arrested who inspired them in their crime,' said Judas. 'They were the Nazarene's men.'

Pilate chewed his lower lip.

'I could not make the arrest,' he said. The situation in Jerusalem was already dangerous, but if they were to arrest this 'king' they might precipitate a full-scale revolt that he would not be able to handle. He wanted trouble, but he did not want to seem to be the cause of it. Tiberius would blame him, not the Jews. However, if the Jews were to make the arrest, it would divert the people's anger away from the Romans sufficiently for the troops to be able to handle matters. The Pharisees must be won over. They must make the arrest. 'Wait here,' he said to Judas. 'I will send a message to Caiaphas.'

And they came to a place which was named Gethsemane: and he saith to his disciples, Sit ye here, while I shall pray. And he taketh with him Peter and James and John, and began to be sore amazed, and to be very heavy; And saith unto them, My soul is exceeding sorrowful unto death: tarry ye here, and watch.

(Mark 14: 32–34)

Glogauer could see the mob approaching now. For the first time since Nazareth he felt physically weak and exhausted.

They were going to kill him. He had to die; he accepted that, but he was afraid of the pain that was to come. He sat down on the ground of the hillside, watching the torches as they came closer.

'The ideal of martyrdom only ever existed in the minds of a few ascetics,' Monica had said. *'Otherwise it was morbid masochism, an easy way to forgo ordinary responsibility, a method of keeping repressed people under control…'*

'It isn't as simple as that…'

'It is, Karl.'

He could show Monica now.

His regret was that she was unlikely ever to know. He had meant to write everything down and put it into the time machine and hope that it would be recovered. It was strange. He was not a religious man in the usual sense. He was an agnostic. It was not conviction that had led him to defend religion against Monica's cynical contempt for it; it was rather lack of conviction in the ideal in which she had set her own faith, the ideal of science as a solver of all problems. He could not share her faith and there was nothing else but religion, though he could not believe in the kind of God of Christianity. The God seen as a mystical force of the mysteries of Christianity and other great religions had not been personal enough for him. His rational mind had told him that God did not exist in any personal form. His unconscious had told him that faith in science was not enough. He remembered the self-contempt he had once felt and wondered why he had felt it.

'Science is basically opposed to religion,' Monica had once said. *'No matter how many Jesuits get together and rationalise their views of science, the fact remains that religion cannot accept the fundamental attitudes of science and it is implicit in science to attack the fundamental principles of religion. The only area in which there is no difference and need be no war is the ultimate assumption. One may or may not assume there is a God. But at soon as one begins to defend one's assumption, there must be strife.'*

'You're talking about organised religion…'

'I'm talking about religion as opposed to belief. Who needs the ritual of religion when we have the far superior ritual of science to replace it? Religion is a reasonable substitute for knowledge. But there is no longer any need for substitutes, Karl. Science offers a sounder basis on which to formulate systems of thought and ethics. We don't need the carrot of heaven and the big stick of hell any more when science can show the consequences of actions and men can judge easily for themselves whether those actions are right or wrong.'

'I can't accept it.'

'That's because you're sick. I'm sick, too, but at least I can see the promise of health.'

'I can only see the threat of death…'

As they had agreed, Judas kissed him on the cheek and the mixed force of Temple guards and Roman soldiers surrounded him.

To the Romans he said, with some difficulty, 'I am the King of the Jews.' To the Pharisees' servants he said: 'I am the messiah who has come to destroy your masters.'

Now he was committed and the final ritual was to begin.

Chapter Nineteen

I T WAS AN untidy trial, an arbitrary mixture of Roman and Jewish law which did not altogether satisfy anyone. The object was accomplished after several conferences between Pontius Pilate and Caiaphas and three attempts to bend and merge their separate legal systems in order to fit the expediencies of the situation. Both needed a scapegoat for their different purposes and so at last the result was achieved and the madman convicted, on the one hand of rebellion against Rome and on the other of heresy.

A peculiar feature of the trial was that the witnesses were all followers of the man and yet seemed eager to see him convicted.

'Ah, these morbid fanatics,' said Pilate. He was content.

The Pharisees agreed that the Roman method of execution would fit the time and the situation best in this case and it was decided to crucify him. The man had prestige, however, so that it would be necessary to use some of the tried Roman methods of humiliation in order to make him into a pathetic and ludicrous figure in the eyes of the pilgrims.

Pilate assured the Pharisees that he would see to it, but he made sure that they signed documents that gave their approval to his actions.

The prisoner seemed almost content, though withdrawn. He had spoken enough during the trial to condemn himself, but had said little in his defence.

It is done.

My life is confirmed.

And the soldiers led him away into the hall, called Praetorium; and they called together the whole band. And they clothed him with purple, and platted a crown of thorns, and put it about his head, And began to salute him, Hail, King of the Jews! And they smote him on the head with a reed, and did spit upon him … And when they had mocked him, they took off the purple from him, and put his own clothes on him, and led him out to crucify him.

(Mark 15: 16–20)

'Oh, Karl, you'll do anything for attention…'
'You're after the limelight, young man…'
'God, Karl, what you'll do to get attention…'

Not now. Not this. It's too noble.

Were the faces laughing at him through the haze of pain?

Was his own face there, a look of ludicrous self-pity in its eyes? His own ghost…?

But they could not rid him of the deep feeling of satisfaction that was there. The first full experience of the kind he had ever had.

His brain was clouded now, by pain and by the ritual humiliation; by his having completely given himself up to his rôle.

He was too weak to bear the heavy wooden cross and he walked behind it as it was dragged towards Golgotha by a Cyrenian whom the Romans had press-ganged for the purpose.

As he staggered through the crowded, silent streets, watched by those who had thought he would lead them against the Roman overlords, his eyes would refuse to focus and he occasionally staggered off the road and was nudged back onto it by one of the Roman guards.

'You are too emotional, Karl. Why don't you use that brain of yours and pull yourself together…?'

He remembered the words, but it was difficult to remember who had said them or who Karl was.

The road that led up the side of the hill was stony and he slipped sometimes, remembering another hill he had climbed. It seemed to him that he had been a child, but the memory merged with the others and it was impossible to know.

He was breathing heavily and with some difficulty. The pain of the thorns in his head was barely felt, but his whole body seemed to throb in unison with his heartbeats. It was like a drum.

It was evening. The sun was setting. He fell on his face, cutting his head on a sharp stone, just as he reached the top of the hill. He fainted.

He had been a child. Was he still a child? They would not murder a child. If he made it plain to them that he was a child...?

And they bring him unto the place Golgotha, which is, being inter-preted, The place of a skull, And they gave him to drink wine mingled with myrrh: but he received it not.

(Mark 15: 22–23)

He knocked the cup aside. The soldier shrugged and reached out for one of his arms. Another soldier already held the other arm.

As he recovered consciousness he began to tremble violently. He felt the pain intensely as the ropes bit into the flesh of his wrists and ankles. He struggled.

He felt something cold placed against his palm. Although it only covered a small area in the centre of his hand it seemed very heavy. He heard a sound that also was a rhythm with his heartbeats. He turned his head to look at the hand. It was a man's hand.

The large iron peg was being driven into the hand by a soldier swinging a mallet as he lay on a heavy wooden cross which was at this moment horizontal on the ground. He watched, wondering why there was no pain. The soldier swung the mallet higher as the peg met the resistance of the wood. Twice he missed the peg and struck the fingers.

He looked to the other side and saw that the second soldier was also hammering in a peg. Evidently he had missed a great many times because the fingers of that hand were bloody and crushed.

The first soldier finished hammering in his peg and turned his attention to the feet.

He felt the iron slide through his flesh, heard it hammering home.

Using a pulley, they began to haul the cross into the vertical position. Glogauer noticed that he was alone. No others were being crucified that day.

The little silver cross, dangling between the breasts, the rough wooden cross advancing.

His erection came and went.

He had a clear view of the lights of Jerusalem below him. There was a little light in the sky, but it was fading.

Soon it would be completely dark.

There was a small crowd looking on. One of the women seemed familiar. He called to her.

'Monica?'

But his voice was cracked and the word was a whisper. The woman did not look up.

He felt his body dragging at the nails which supported it. He thought he felt a twinge of pain in his left hand. He seemed to be bleeding heavily.

It was odd, he reflected, that it should be him hanging here. He supposed that it was the event he had originally come to witness. There was little doubt, really. Everything had gone perfectly.

The pain in his left hand increased.

He glanced down at the Roman guards who were playing dice at the foot of the cross. He smiled. They were absorbed in their game. He could not see the markings of the dice from this distance.

He sighed. The movement of his chest seemed to throw extra strain on his hands. The pain was quite bad now. He winced and tried somehow to ease himself back against the wood.

He was breathing with difficulty. The pain began to spread through his body. He gritted his teeth. It was dreadful. He gasped and shouted. He writhed.

There was no longer any light in the sky. Heavy clouds obscured stars and moon.

From below came whispered voices.

'Let me down,' he called. 'Oh, please let me down!'

I am only a little boy.

'Fuck off, you bitch!'

The pain filled him. He was gasping rapidly for air. He slumped forward, but nobody released him.

A little while later he raised his head. The movement caused a return of the agony and again he began to writhe on the cross. He was being slowly asphyxiated.

'Let me down. Please. Please stop it!'

Every part of his flesh, every muscle and tendon and bone of him, was filled with impossible pain.

He knew he would not survive until the next day as he had thought he might.

And at the ninth hour Jesus cried with a loud voice, saying, 'Eloi, Eloi, lama sabachthani?' which is, being interpreted, My God, my God, why hast thou forsaken me?

(Mark 15: 34)

Glogauer coughed. It was a dry, barely heard sound. The soldiers below the cross heard it because the night was now so quiet.

'It's funny,' said one. 'Yesterday they were worshipping the bastard. Today they seemed to want to kill him – even the ones who were closest to him.'

'I'll be glad when we get out of this country,' said his companion.

They shouldn't kill a child, he thought.

He heard Monica's voice again. 'It's weakness and fear, Karl, that's driven you to this. Martyrdom is a conceit.'

He coughed once more and the pain returned, but it was duller now. His breathing was becoming more shallow.

Just before he died he began to talk again, muttering the words until his breath was gone. 'It's a lie – it's a lie – it's a lie…'

Later, after his body was stolen by the servants of some doctors who believed it might have special properties, there were rumours that he had not died. But the corpse was already rotting in the doctors' dissecting rooms and would soon be destroyed.

MICHAEL MOORCOCK (1939–) is one of the most important figures in British SF and Fantasy literature. The author of many literary novels and stories in practically every genre, he has won and been shortlisted for numerous awards including the Hugo, Nebula, World Fantasy, Whitbread and Guardian Fiction Prize. He is also a musician who performed in the seventies with his own band, the Deep Fix; and, as a member of the space-rock band, Hawkwind, won a platinum disc. His tenure as editor of NEW WORLDS magazine in the sixties and seventies is seen as the high watermark of SF editorship in the UK, and was crucial in the development of the SF New Wave. Michael Moorcock's literary creations include Hawkmoon, Corum, Von Bek, Jerry Cornelius and, of course, his most famous character, Elric. He has been compared to, among others, Balzac, Dumas, Dickens, James Joyce, Ian Fleming, J.R.R. Tolkien and Robert E. Howard. Although born in London, he now splits his time between homes in Texas and Paris.

For a more detailed biography, please see Michael Moorcock's entry in *The Encyclopedia of Science Fiction* at: http://www.sf-encyclopedia.com/

For further information about Michael Moorcock and his work, please visit www.multiverse.org, or send S.A.E. to The Nomads Of The Time Streams, Mo Dhachaidh, Loch Awe, Dalmally, Argyll, PA33 1AQ, Scotland, or P.O. Box 385716, Waikoloa, HI 96738, USA.